Mo...

MURDER IN THE PLACE OF ANUBIS

"MURDER IN THE PLACE OF ANUBIS is the debut of a marvelous new talent. Robinson's evocation of time and place is a vivid travelogue, her characters come to three-dimensional life, and her detective, Lord Meren, deduces with the best of them. It's going to be a pleasure to introduce readers to Lynda Robinson. I'm already looking forward to the next one."

> —STEVEN STILWELL
> Once Upon a Crime (Minneapolis)

"For those looking for something different, this is one that will be enjoyed."

> —Rendezvous

"Trust us on this one. . . . You gotta like a mystery where the Sam Spade is Lord Meren, the 'Eyes and Ears' of Pharaoh Tutankhamun."

> —MFE Collectors' BookLine

MURDER IN THE PLACE OF ANUBIS

Lynda S. Robinson

BALLANTINE BOOKS • NEW YORK

Copyright © 1994 by Lynda S. Robinson

All rights reserved under International and Pan-American Copyright Conventions. Published in the United States of America by Ballantine Books, a division of Random House, Inc., New York, and distributed in Canada by Random House of Canada Limited, Toronto.

No part of this book may be reproduced or transmitted in any form or by any means, electronic or mechanical, including photocopying, recording, or by any information storage and retrieval system, without permission in writing from the publisher.

With the exception of recognized historical figures and incidents, all characters and events portrayed in this work are fictitious.

Library of Congress Catalog Card Number: 93-26878

ISBN 0-345-38922-0

This edition is published by arrangement with Walker and Company.

Manufactured in the United States of America

First Ballantine Books Edition: February 1995

10 9 8 7 6 5 4 3 2

Most writers have at least one person who inspires them, cheers them on, and supports them. I have someone like that, someone who risked with me, fought my battles with me, and believed in me. There are no words that can express my gratitude and my love. Wess Robinson, this dedication, and everything I write, is for you.

$\triangledown$

1

Year Five of the Reign of the Pharaoh Tutankhamun

Year Five of the Reign of the Pharaoh Tutankhamun

There were seven bodies ready to be taken out of the natron, and the priest Raneb was anxious to see that his customer was the first to be bandaged. The widower of Lady Shapu had given Raneb a bronze vase to ensure that his wife's embalming was perfect. Raneb knew how careless the bandagers became after wrapping the dead with resin-soaked linen all day. Lady Shapu was going to be first.

Marshaling his flock of water carriers, fire stokers, bandagers, and unguent mixers, Raneb bustled along an avenue formed by mountains of natron, the salt used to dry a corpse. In the distance priests and laborers made their way to the shelters where new bodies awaited sweetening in a wash of natron and water.

As Raneb entered the drying shed, he consulted a sheet of papyrus containing a list of the dead, their dates of lustration and drying, and the name of the lector priest in charge of each. Before him lay a double row of alabaster embalming tables heaped with natron. The surface of each table was concave to allow the fluids that drained from a corpse to collect in funnels that emptied into stone bowls at either end of the table.

1

Raneb marched down the central aisle, tailed by his covey of assistants. He muttered to himself.

"Thuya, son of Penno, Lady Hathor." Raneb halted and consulted a tag attached to one of the tables. "Prince Seti." He shook his head and passed on to the next table. "Ah! Lady Shapu, priestess of . . . priestess of . . . Oh yes, priestess of the goddess Isis."

Folding his papyrus, Raneb turned to the men behind him. One of them yawned.

"Close your mouth," Raneb said. "Have reverence for the work of Anubis. You look as if we should put you in the natron along with Lady Shapu."

"I beg pardon, Lector Priest Raneb."

Raneb grunted, then pointed at the natron table. "This is the one." He pulled a rolled papyrus from his belt. "No, you fool, don't start shoveling until I'm ready. Let me find the prayer. Here it is."

Raneb frowned at one of the bandagers, who was shuffling his feet. The man stood still and fixed his eyes on the ground.

"Lord Everlasting who hast died and risen again, Lord Osiris, ruler of the dead . . ."

Raneb nodded at the bandager named Pashed without ceasing his chant. The man stepped up to the natron table holding a wooden shovel. Sinking it in the crystals, he hit a solid object. Raneb raised his brows, but continued chanting. He could have sworn Lady Shapu had been placed much deeper.

Pashed nudged the obstruction gently, shrugged, and began scraping away the natron from a leg. A pale, thick calf appeared. Pashed halted, and Raneb forgot to chant his spell. After forty days in natron, a body was almost black, the arms and legs shrunk to kindling.

Letting the papyrus roll snap closed, Raneb made a sound like a jackal robbed of its prey. "Sufferings of

Isis! Who has dumped a stranger on top of my Lady Shapu? You, and you, don't stand about gawking, get this intruder out. His essence will mix with the lady's."

Raneb began to circle the natron table. "I'm tired of all these mistakes and carelessness. The Controller of the Mysteries is going to hear of this."

Pashed and his fellows scrambled onto the edge of the table and began shoveling. Feet appeared. Discolored natron shifted to reveal a stained kilt. Pashed wrinkled his nose at the odor of feces that arose when the garment was uncovered. Beside Pashed, the fire stoker brushed crystals from the head of a man. Uttering a curse, the fire stoker leapt backward off the table. Raneb scowled at the acrobatics, but the fire stoker pointed a shaking finger at the head of the corpse. Raneb came nearer.

Dusted with a coat of natron, webbed with the fine wrinkles of middle age, the neck of the intruder was as pale as the rest of the body. And from the flesh of the throat protruded an obsidian embalming knife.

Meren heard a scream. A jolt of pain lanced through the flesh of his wrist, up his arm to his heart, and he shot upright, panting. The war-drum beat of his pulse hammered in his temples as he clutched his hands in the bedding and stared at the gauzy curtains beyond the bed. Slowly, he drew a bare leg up against his chest and hugged it.

The nightmare had come to him again, when he'd thought his heart free of the terror. Perhaps it was the *ka* of the dead king that wouldn't free him. He'd been back in that cell again, confused and alone, his stomach in knots from its emptiness, his back a mass of welts from the beatings. All because his father refused to cast out the old gods of Egypt for Pharaoh's god of the sun disk.

"No." Meren squeezed his eyes shut, but he was too late to stop the memory from invading his thoughts.

He was back in the cell again, and they'd come to kill him, but he didn't care anymore. He was eighteen, and he welcomed death, for they'd made his body a vessel of torment. He would join Osiris in the netherworld. Meren lay on his stomach on the packed earth floor. Naked, his back caked with dried blood, he watched dirty feet march toward him, stop, and shift to stand beside his arms. He bit his lip to stop from whimpering when the guards pulled him up. He wobbled on his feet, and they had to support him so that he remained standing. They dragged him out of the cell into another where shadows danced in the light cast by torches.

A cold hand touched his face, and Meren opened his eyes. Akhenaten stared at him with his rabid black eyes. Meren smiled at the king, amused that Pharaoh would think it fitting to watch him die. His position as heir of one of the oldest noble families in Egypt had gotten him thrown into a cell in the first place, and now it would bring him death in the presence of the living god.

"I should kill you as I did your father," the king said. The cold hand toyed with a lock of Meren's hair. "But Ay speaks on your behalf. He says you're young enough to be taught the truth. My majesty thinks not, but the One God, my Father, commands me to be merciful to our children. Isn't that so, Ay?"

"Yes, Divine One."

Meren blinked and swiveled his head. Ay had been beside him all along. Meren pulled his eyelids open wide in an effort to see his mentor. Ay's narrow face blurred and then sharpened, and Meren sucked in his breath. Ay caught his gaze and held it.

The king spoke again. "We will ask once, Lord

Meren. Do you accept the Aten, my Father, as the one true god?"

Meren stared into the eyes of his mentor and gave his head a slight shake. Ay was asking him to bring damnation upon his *ka*. Father had died rather than risk his eternal soul; could he do less? But Ay wanted him to live. Meren could see it in his eyes. And may the gods forgive him, Meren wanted to live.

Meren opened his cracked lips and said in a voice that was hoarse from screaming, "The Aten is the one true god, as thy majesty has pronounced."

Ay nodded to him, but the movement was so slight that Meren could have imagined it.

"Words come easily for you," the king said. "But my Father has shown me a way to claim your *ka* for the truth. Bring him."

The guards dragged him after the king farther into the cell. They stopped before a man crouched behind a glowing brazier. Meren's vision filled with the red and white glow of the fire. Before he could protest, he was thrown to the floor on his back. This time he couldn't stop the cry that burst from him as his scored flesh hit the ground. A heavy, sweating body landed on his chest. Meren arched, trying to throw the man off, but the guard was twice his weight.

His face was turned toward the brazier. Beside it he could see the fine pleats of Pharaoh's robe and the edge of a gold sandal as he fought to keep the guards from spreading his right arm out. In spite of his resistance, the arm was caught and pinned so that his palm was up. A guard knelt on his upper arm, making it go numb. The man behind the brazier lifted a white-hot brand and approached Meren.

He couldn't see his arm because the guard was kneeling on it. He felt a wet cloth wipe the flesh of his wrist, saw the brand lift in the air. It was the sun disk, the Aten, the circle with sticklike rays extending from it and ending in stylized hands. The glowing sun disk poised in the air, then descended quickly as the guard set the hot metal to Meren's arm.

There was a brief moment between the time the brand met his flesh and the first agony. During that instant, Meren smelled for the first time the odor of burning flesh. Then he screamed. Seared flesh screamed along with him. Every muscle he had spasmed while the guard held the brand to his wrist. When it was taken away, Meren's whole body broke out in a sweat. He shivered as the pain from his wrist rolled over him.

He lost consciousness briefly, and when he opened his eyes, the men who held him were gone. The one who had branded him was smearing a salve on his burned flesh. The pain receded. Hands lifted him to face the king. Akhenaten's black fire eyes burned into him as no brand ever could. Pharaoh took Meren's hand, turned it to expose the mutilated wrist, examined the crimson symbol of his god. He placed Meren's hand in Ay's.

"He is yours now. But remember, my majesty will know if the boy is false. If he falters from the true path, he dies."

He dies. Meren covered his ears to block out the voice he still remembered after sixteen years. He twisted, lifted his legs, and set his feet on the cool tiles of the floor. Standing, he took three steps, swept aside the filmy curtains that sheltered his bed, and stepped down from the dais. Moonlight spilled into the room from the open door that led to the reflection pool. Meren went out into the garden and knelt by the water. He dipped his hands in it and splashed his face. His eye caught the white scar on his wrist, and he quickly turned his arm so that he couldn't see it. Sometimes the old wound would itch for no reason, and he would go through torture trying not to touch it. He never touched it unless he had to.

Returning to his chamber, Meren went directly to the niche where the statue of the god Osiris rested. He knelt and said a prayer in which he begged the god to intercede for him with the other gods. That done, he turned to a casket inlaid with turquoise and ivory, took three leather balls from it, and tossed them, one after the other, into the air. The spheres sailed up and down. The only sound he listened to was the soft pat of the leather hitting his palms.

He'd tried magic charms to ward off dream demons. He had once tried his physician's sleeping draught. He had tried wearing himself out with a woman. Then his son had given him the leather balls, and Meren had discovered peace. He couldn't think of anything else if he wanted those spheres to stay in the air.

Faster and faster he tossed the balls, until his heart was filled with the motion of his hands and the flight of the small missiles. Gradually his breathing slowed and the strung-bow feeling left him.

Once he was calm, he heard the rapid slap of bare feet on the floor outside his room. Meren caught the balls and put them on the floor. He went still, straining to catch the direction of the sound. Slithering to the opening that led to the courtyard, Meren put his back to the wall and edged around the door.

In the shadow of a palm tree he spotted a black figure, which stooped and picked up something with both hands. Meren smiled when the intruder straightened and almost tottered backward. A honey pot clutched to his protruding belly, mouth screwed up in concentration on his task, the son of his son dipped a fist into the vessel and jammed it into his mouth.

Meren called softly, "Remi."

Remi looked up, saw Meren, and grinned a sticky grin. Meren laughed. Striding to the child, he picked him up and rested the boy on his hip. The honey pot jammed into Meren's stomach, and Remi shoved it in front of his face. Rescuing the pot, Meren squeezed the child to him.

"Greedy little bee, you're the first one up as usual."

Oblivious to the slumbering quiet of the household, Remi began to chatter in a loud voice. "I want to play, and I can't find my bow and arrows. Nurse hid them."

"Quiet! If you're good, you may watch me juggle."

Meren went back to his room with the boy in tow. Remi was his best audience for juggling. Count Meren, Friend of the King, one of Pharaoh's confidential intelligencers, couldn't forgo his dignity in public by juggling like a common entertainer. Kysen had long since lost patience with watching Meren's antics, but Kysen's son had not.

Setting Remi on the floor with his honey pot, Meren took up the juggling balls once more. As he tossed them from one hand to the other, the first light of dawn filtered into the room. Often—when he was troubled over what mischief the Hittites were up to with Pharaoh's Syrian vassals, or whether the death of a rich Babylonian merchant was an accident or murder—he would put aside his worries and juggle, only to find that turning his thoughts away from the problem had somehow helped him see it differently.

He needed the serenity that tossing the spheres brought; soon he would wash, dress, and go to the palace to attend Pharaoh. A gold band would cover his wrist, blocking from the king's sight the mark put there by Tutankhamun's brother. For the king could bear the sight no more than could Meren; it was a reminder of madness, of near civil war, and of death.

The honey pot sailed at him. Meren dropped a ball and snatched the jar. It bounced in his hand. A sphere hit his head. Another hit his foot, but he kept hold of the honey pot. Brown goo spilled over his hand and through his fingers. Remi crowed, and Meren danced out of the way of a stream of honey. Righting the jar, Meren set it on the floor and wiped his hands on the lip.

"You little demon, for that you must pay. You'll shower with me." Remi turned over from his sitting position, climbed to his feet, and started running. Meren caught him at the door. "Got you. Where's your nurse? Did you put her in a clothing chest? Lock her in with the cattle?" His answer was a smirking giggle.

With Remi in his arms, Meren walked out into the courtyard and headed for the women's quarters. As he passed the dining hall, he heard pounding at the front door. It had to be loud to reach him through the dining hall, reception chamber, and entryway. Servants were stirring; a maid ran up to take Remi from him. Meren was heading back to his room to bathe away the honey that coated his hands when the old man who served as his porter scurried up to him.

Bowing, the man rubbed his hands on his kilt. "Pardon, lord, pardon, pardon."

Meren stopped and waited patiently. It did no good to lose patience with old Seti. He only panicked.

"You know I don't want to see anyone until after I've dined with my son and Remi." Meren turned away.

"Pardon, lord. It is a priest, an embalmer priest." Seti made a sign against evil and lowered his voice. "He seeks help, lord, for there has been a murder in the Place of Anubis."

* * *

Meren held out his hand for the king's falcon collar. Gold, turquoise, and malachite bead strands curled into his palm, and he stepped back with his eyes lowered. The king stood with his arms at his sides, his gaze fixed on the double doors of his robing chamber. His lips pressed together so hard that their fullness almost disappeared. One hand clenched and unclenched around the belt that secured his kilt.

Since Pharaoh hadn't given permission for anyone to speak, the loudest sounds in the room were the click of gold against stone and the rustle of pleated linen. Meren took an engraved electrum armband from a casket and handed it to the vizier Ay. The king's arm shot out, stiff, the hand balled in a fist. Ay fastened the hinged band. The arm swung down. At the same time a muscle in Pharaoh's jaw twitched. Meren offered the matching band to Ay; he looked up at the king's face. As he did so, Tutankhamun abandoned his pretense of studying the door and looked at him. Meren winked, and the king's solar smile burst upon him.

"The Lord Meren has permission to speak to my majesty," the king said.

Meren tried not to look at the vizier. Refusing to allow his chief minister to speak was one of the king's small vengeances taken upon the man who was his foster father. It served Ay right for piling too many duties on a boy who was only fourteen, for all he was the son of the god. This morning Ay had foiled the king's attempt to steal from the palace and sail his skiff on the Nile. Instead, Pharaoh spent the morning in ceremony and listening to the avaricious howling of the priests of Amun.

"Sovereign, my master, what is thy will?"

Tutankhamun grinned at Meren while holding out his

hand so that Ay could slide a ring on it. "You are one of the Eyes and Ears of Pharaoh. What happenings are there to report?"

"Nubian bandits in the south, majesty. And the prince who absconded with the serfs of Lord Soter has been persuaded to return them."

"Prince Hunefer would rob the night of its stars if he could," Tutankhamun said. He twisted one of the rings on his hand.

"And there has been murder, divine lord."

The king lifted his eyes from the ring. He waved his hand; servants and lords faded away through the double doors.

"Tell me."

Meren hesitated for the space of a heartbeat, during which he stifled his own guilt. He would be commanded to hunt a murderer again, when he was guilty of that crime himself. No matter that he hadn't known they were going to kill Akhenaten. He'd suspected it and let Ay send him to the Libyan border anyway. And even if his own conscience were clear, he worried about the boy king. There was no way of knowing whether his news would bring out the youth in Pharaoh, or the burdened monarch.

"A man has been found in the Place of Anubis," Meren said. "He was stabbed in the neck with an embalming knife, and the Controller of the Mysteries of Anubis begs me for aid."

The king's eyes grew round. He rested a knee on the seat of an ebony chair and shivered. "Desecration of the place of embalming. Do you—do you think that the poor souls of the dead ones have fled in fear? They might be afraid to be reborn."

"I don't know, majesty, but this evil touches a sacred

place and involves priests. One must not capture suspicious ones and beat them in hope of finding a criminal."

"No," the king said. "It isn't wise to beat priests."

Tutankhamun turned and slouched down in the ebony chair. "You're going to hunt another murderer, and I will sit for hours in the throne room listening to the complaints of governors, bureaucrats, priests, and that cobra of a Hittite ambassador."

Meren bowed to his king. He took in the wistful expression and slumped shoulders. Once Kysen had been burdened as was the king, and it had taken Meren years to undo the damage wrought by his adopted son's natural father. He would speak to Ay about allowing the king time to be a youth instead of a divine ruler.

"I sent my son to the Place of Anubis before I attended Pharaoh. Shall I come to the sovereign with news of this abomination?"

"Yes!" The king jumped from the chair. It went sliding across the floor. "Yes, tell me everything. At least I can trust you not to conceal the evil from me or dress up your affairs in order to gain favor. You must hurry. This matter of the embalming knife is likely to be the only interesting business of the day."

It was Meren who jumped when Pharaoh grabbed his arm and hauled him toward the doors. Tutankhamun flung open the door and gave Meren's shoulder a push.

"Hurry. I remember what you told me: One must study the place where evil has been done before the scent and markings of that evil vanish. Hurry."

Meren stepped out of the royal suite. The door banged shut, and he looked around at the astonished courtiers, who regarded him as if he were a red crocodile. Hiding the consternation that had gripped him since Pharaoh touched him, Meren ducked behind a column and set off for his chariot. News of that touch would be all over the court in an hour. By nightfall, word of the sign of favor would be on its way to Babylon, Tyre, Sidon, the courts of the Syrian princes, and the king of the Hittites.

As he threaded his way through the crowds of nobles, civil servants, and palace dignitaries, Meren maintained what he liked to call his unseen mask. Having spent many years in a court where a smile at the wrong person or the lifting of a brow at the wrong time could mean death, concealing the true face of his *ka*, his soul, was as natural as wearing a kilt. Before the old Pharaoh killed his father, he'd been as open as a lotus blossom. The day Pharaoh's guards took his father away, the bloom closed up into a tight knot and never reopened. Within the knot he concealed the scars of his father's death, his own torture and degradation—and the suspected truth about Akhenaten's death.

Living with the scars was easier now. As with the scar from his branding, the surface injuries had long since healed. Only occasionally, as this morning, did he suffer from visitations from the past. Did the gods know, and send the memories to haunt him as a warning of coming evil? It was as if they cautioned him to be fair, to seek out Maat, the essential truth and harmony of life by which the world existed. But could he? Once he had confused the good of the country with his own need for vengeance and allowed a man to die.

No, that wasn't true. Others had decided that there had been enough madness in the Two Lands long before Meren suspected a movement to kill Akhenaten. If he had tried to stop them, they would have killed him too. Ay put no one above the good of Egypt.

Meren shook his head in an attempt to clear it of conflicting principles. An old battle, this one. He sometimes imagined himself in the Hall of Judgment in the netherworld, standing before the eternal scales while the gods weighed his heart against the feather of truth. The scales would teeter back and forth. They would sway wildly until the pan that held his heart clattered to the floor. His heart would burst open and swarms of maggots spill out of it, and the gods would condemn him to be devoured by monsters.

Meren, you have the wits of a porcupine. He deliberately turned his thoughts back to the court and the king.

To survive he'd learned to wear unseen masks, facades constructed to suit his purpose of the moment. It was a skill taught him by his father and the vizier, and it was one he was attempting to pass on to the king. For a trusting, open sovereign courted destruction.

Meren allowed himself a barely audible sigh. It wouldn't be long before the king realized the consequences of that open display of favor. Meren already knew that in those short moments he had acquired many new enemies and false friends. One of the king's ancestors had written something about the court. He'd advised his son not to trust a brother or know a friend, and when lying down to guard his heart himself. Meren had always remembered that advice, along with the caution that in Pharaoh's court, even the king has no friends on the day of woe.

2

It took less than an hour for Meren and several of the royal charioteers who were his assistants to drive to the Place of Anubis. During the trip down the southern road from the palace on the west bank, Meren packed away his doubts in the sealed casket of his *ka*. He'd indulged in the luxury of self-reproach too long. Pharaoh's justice must be served, his subjects protected from evil, killers stalked and caught. And by doing so, Meren might assuage the yammering hyenas of his own conscience.

The embalmers' workshops were placed some distance from the palace, government, and mortuary complexes of western Thebes so that the fumes and waste produced by the mysteries wouldn't disturb Pharaoh and his subjects. As he handed the reins of his horses to a groom, Meren wrinkled his nose. He saw that one of his men was making the sign against evil. Kysen was waiting for him in the embalming shed. As usual, his son was prowling about like a hunting hound. Ignoring the grand lector priest, Kysen bombarded an unfortunate bandager with questions. It was the same with each inquiry. Kysen would drop into conversation with the serf, the artisan, the laborer. Only reluctantly would he spar with a lord or a priest. Meren had tried to wean his son of this preference, but it was hard to wipe out the memories of being sold into slavery by a father, even if one did end up the adopted son of a Friend of the King.

Meren received the greetings of the lector priest while perusing the scene. Teams of embalmers went about their chores with little sign that they feared the presence of a soul dispatched from its body in violence. The drying shed was a long tunnel filled by two rows of embalming tables reserved for the wealthier citizens, who could afford the more expensive process of preservation. Along the edge of the open, roofed structure lay tables laden with the tools of the embalmer's craft—spoons, knives, probes, needles, and thread, all in boxes or on trays. An ornate table set apart from the others held a casket carved with hieroglyphs and the image of the jackal god Anubis. The lid of the casket was askew.

Squatting near the casket, looking miserable and frightened, was a young laborer. Meren could scent fear as a hound scents a wounded gazelle. His curiosity was roused, but he knew better than to let it loose. Kysen was in charge, and his son had left the youth by himself for a reason.

Having responded politely to the formal words of the lector priest's greeting, Meren followed the man to the fourth embalming table on the left row. As he approached, Kysen dismissed the laborer he was questioning with a nod. Meren was proud of that nod. It was one of the first signs that the boy had accepted his new position in the world when Kysen first used the gesture of acknowledgment of a noble to a commoner.

Meren and Kysen met at the natron table. Immediately and without words, they fell into their working habits. Like a skilled artisan and his best apprentice, they worked and thought in complementary directions. Kysen knew what tasks Meren would want done; Meren sensed when Kysen needed direction or advice. Standing side by side, they gazed down at the body nestled in the crystals.

"They haven't touched him since they found the knife," Kysen said. "You're here earlier than I expected."

"Pharaoh commanded me to hurry."

Kysen sucked in a breath, then let it out slowly. "The living god is wise."

"The living god is bored." It was difficult not to smile at Kysen's awe. "Don't wheeze as though you had swallowed a whole pomegranate. Tell me what you know."

"This man is Hormin, scribe of records and tithes in the office of the vizier." Kysen nodded in the direction of the frightened laborer. "As they were digging him out, that water carrier recognized him." He pointed to an engraved bronze bracelet on the wrist of the dead man. "Then the lector priest found his name and titles on that. There are also a signet ring and wig."

Kysen leaned over the natron table and touched the obsidian blade that protruded from Hormin's neck. "This is a ritual embalming knife. It is used to make incisions when the bowels—"

"I understand," Meren said. "And this Hormin, is he known to the embalmers?"

"No, only the water carrier admits to having seen him before. I'm going to talk to him after we get rid of the body and that pigeon-witted lector priest."

Kysen shoved away from the natron table and walked over to the side of the shed, and Meren followed. Kysen stopped beside the table containing the Anubis casket.

"The knife was kept in here," he said. He took a blade from the casket. Even in the shade of the embalming shed the facets of the black glass reflected light. Kysen pointed to the ground around the table.

"Blood has soaked into the earth. You can see the stains beneath the footprints, and some of it splattered on the legs of the table. The evil one couldn't remove all the markings in the darkness. I think Hormin was killed here and put on the nearest table that contained enough natron to cover him."

"Very well. Shall we dig Hormin out of his nest?"

Meren stood at the head of the natron table while Kysen supervised the removal of the body. Hormin was lifted onto a carrying board, and two assistants began dusting crystals from the corpse. Kysen withdrew the knife to the accompaniment of a prayer by Raneb. Meren stopped the priest from carrying the blade away.

"Lector, you may have the body after my physician sees it, but I will take the possessions and this blade."

"But it must be purified," Raneb said.

"After I have found the one who killed this man."

The priest bowed, and Meren turned back to the natron table. The two men were shoveling natron away from the darkened remains of Lady Shapu. Kysen jumped down from the table, and Meren shoved an arm in front of his son.

"Don't move," Meren said. He bent down and picked up something from beside his son's foot. He held it out in his palm.

Raneb came over to them and looked at the small stone in Meren's hand. "An *ib* amulet. We have hundreds of them. This one is carved from carnelian. Some are of lapis lazuli, and some are of gold. One of the bandagers must have dropped it."

Meren closed his hand over the amulet. Such talismans were vital to both living and dead, for they protected the wearer's heart, the seat of emotions and intellect. This amulet wasn't made to be suspended from a necklace. Perhaps Raneb was correct, and it was one that belonged in the Place of Anubis.

Meren gave the amulet to Kysen. "Put it with the possessions of Hormin. Don't worry, priest, it will be returned. Lighten your heart. After all, I'm giving the body back to you."

"That is of no comfort, my lord. We will have to say spells and prayers for weeks to rid the area of evil."

Four men lifted the carrying board and body. As they passed Meren lifted a hand to stop them. Meren sniffed. He bent over the corpse, lifted a fold of the man's kilt, and sniffed again. Through the mingled smells of natron and body waste released at death he detected a faint, sweet odor—perfume. On the linen there were light yellow smears. Dropping the kilt, Meren touched the signet ring on Hormin's right hand. It bore engraved hieroglyphs that spelled Hormin's name. Meren straightened and waved the bearers on.

"Kysen, see that they remove everything from the body. I'm going to the offices of the vizier, and then to the house of Hormin. I'll see you after I've finished there."

Meren received his son's respectful inclination of the head. Unspoken was the knowledge that each of them looked forward to their end-of-the-day talk, when they would go over each event, every conversation, winnowing through contrived and honest appearance in search of Maat—order and truth. Leaving Kysen to harry the unhappy Raneb and his fellow priests, Meren and his men drove back to the palace district, away from the realm of the dead.

When a man was murdered in a sacred place, it was the concern of the Eyes and Ears of Pharaoh. When that man was also a servant of the king, the crime merited the scrutiny of the hereditary prince, master of secrets of the Lord of the Two Lands, privy councillor and Friend of the King, Meren, Lord of the Thinite Nome. And because the evil touched the business of the king, Meren went first to the office of the vizier.

Instead of looking for the records and tithes office where the man Hormin had worked, Meren went first to a room filled with stacks of papyri and swarming with clerks. At a table on a raised dais sat an elderly man whose hands were swollen at the joints. The skin of his palms and fingers was soft and permanently stained with red and black ink. Meren approached, sending clerks scurrying out of his way by walking steadily forward without looking to see if anyone was in his path.

The old man looked up from a papyrus when Meren routed three of the men hovering over his table. The old man returned to his papyrus and barked at Meren, "Quick, boy, what is immortality?"

Meren smiled and said, "A book, for though a man's body is dust, and all his kin perish, his words make him remembered through the mouth of the storyteller."

"Adequate," the old man said. He shoved his papyrus at one of the clerks. "Come here, lad, and tell me what brings the Friend of Pharaoh to his old teacher."

A chair appeared in the hands of one of the scribes. The man set it near his master, but Meren only leaned on its back. "Master Ahmose, there is trouble."

"And there is sand in the desert and water in the Nile. Your *ka* draws trouble as a whore attracts sailors."

"I don't seek out trouble."

"Your father was of like spirit, and that's why the Heretic killed him. At least you learned from his example."

At the mention of his father, Meren lowered his eyes. Removing a hand from the chair, he touched the tips of his fingers to the bronze dagger in his belt. The cold metal eased his *ka*, and he lifted his eyes once more.

Ahmose was watching him. "You've learned much."

"I'm not a youth anymore. Master Ahmose, I would speak with you about one of your officials. Hormin, a scribe of records and tithes. He has been murdered in the Place of Anubis."

"I know. One of the priests came to tell me."

Ahmose got up and stepped down from the dais. Meren joined him, and they walked out into a courtyard. Ahmose took refuge from the sun on a stool under a sycamore beside a reflection pool. Meren sat at his feet.

"Well, boy, why are you looking for the killer? Hormin was a contentious man, a plump goose stuffed with hatred and basted with rancor. There's no need to search out one who has relieved so many of a vicious annoyance."

Meren shook his head and studied a yellow fish in the reflection pool. "Murder is a sin against Maat, the divine order of justice and rightness. You taught me about Maat, and now you want me to allow an offense against the harmony of Pharaoh's kingdom?"

"Hormin was an offense in himself," Ahmose said. "I know you, Meren. You won't stop until you've conducted inquiries, pursued the lion into the desert, brought down the waterfowl with your throw stick. But think on this. No matter how many rebels you subdue or criminals you banish into the desert, you'll never right the injustice done against your father."

Meren rose and faced Ahmose. "Are you going to tell me whom I should question, or will I have to spend days speaking to each man in the office of records and tithes?"

Using a black-smudged finger, Ahmose traced the hieroglyph of the *ka*.

"Hormin's skin was always shining," Ahmose said. "As if he were a sack into which someone had poured oil that leaked out. He had a habit of digging his smallest finger in his ear when he talked, and he didn't bathe enough. For these faults alone I would have dispatched the man. Here, boy, don't go away. I'll tell you what you need to know. His younger son, Djaper, works as his apprentice. Quick as a leopard is that one, and has the tongue of a courtier. Though where he got it, considering his sire, I don't know."

"Where is the son?"

Ahmose picked up a sycamore leaf from the ground and crumpled it between his fingers. "Sent word he'd be late this morning. He didn't say why, but after the Anubis priest came, I understood. As for the rest who worked with Hormin, there's one man who fought with him all the time. Came to blows, they did. His name is Bakwerner, and he's in charge of the scribes of the fields of the Lord of the Two Lands. Take my advice, lad, you don't want to know any more about Hormin than you already do."

"Master, I'm going to find this criminal. Was Hormin here all day yesterday?"

"A waste of your time." Ahmose glanced at Meren's shuttered features. "You always were tenacious, like a crocodile. Yesterday? I sent Hormin on an errand to the temple of Amun, more to get rid of him for a while than for any real need. And later someone told me he had to go to the village of the tomb makers to hunt that concubine. Stupid man. Concubines cost, and they make trouble."

Meren was standing beside Ahmose with his thumbs stuck in his belt. "The village of the tomb makers." He hoped his voice was steady. It wouldn't do to reveal his apprehension at the master's words. "I'll find out what he did while he was away. Thank you, master."

"It's nothing, boy. You're going to have a time sorting out Hormin's enemies. Pharaoh's enemies now. I understand you must hunt them, or spar with the Hittite ambassador. This other is unimportant."

"Murder is never unimportant."

Ahmose snorted, and Meren gave up justifying himself to his former teacher. Even the squabbles of three daughters never troubled his *ka* as did this man who refused to see that he was no longer a youth to be chastised and guided. From Ahmose he had learned the art of writing, of manipulation of numbers. It was from his old tutor that he caught the obsession with the writings of the ancestors, and it was Ahmose's fault that Meren quoted texts as a judge spouts law.

"Sit down, boy, and I'll tell you more of Hormin."

Sighing, Meren gave up the idea of trying to get Ahmose to stop calling him "boy," and sat down as he was ordered.

The office of records and tithes was in a separate building not far from the vizier's domain. In front of it was a survey team consisting of scribes, inspectors, measurers, and their boy assistants. It was near the season called Harvest, and Pharaoh's scribes scoured the land assessing taxes.

Meren stepped out of the sun and into the cool shade of the porch that surrounded the records office. On the floor sat five boys grinding pigment, mixing ink, and smoothing the surface of fresh papyrus sheets. Until Meren appeared, they had been laughing and joking among themselves. As Meren walked by, grinding stones rubbed faster, smoothing stones pressed harder. His assistants stopped at the door.

Inside, Meren came upon an unusual scene. In the middle of a room lined with shelves from floor to roof clustered a group of men. Each held a pottery cup, and one of them was pouring from a wine jar. Meren stopped inside the door and listened to the man pouring the wine.

"I know we all prayed to the good god Amun for deliverance, but who among us has had his supplication answered so quickly?"

"Do you think master Ahmose will take Djaper as his assistant now?" another man asked. "We've all seen how much he favors him."

A third laughed and nearly spilled his wine. "The only reason Djaper wasn't favored before was because the master would have had to elevate Hormin. Watch yourself, Bakwerner, Djaper is free of the carrion that was tied to his ankle."

"You're a pig, Montu," said the wine pourer. He looked up from his task, saw Meren, and shut his mouth. The others joined him in staring. At once they all splintered in different directions and left the wine pourer to face Meren. Setting the jar on the floor, the man approached, bowed, and muttered a greeting that acknowledged Meren by name.

"I would see the man called Bakwerner," Meren said.

"I am he, my lord."

Meren strolled over to a shelf, and Bakwerner was forced to follow him. Taking out a papyrus, Meren unrolled it and studied the cursive hieroglyphs that covered the paper.

"Why would you want the scribe Hormin dead?" Meren prided himself on his skill at flushing waterfowl from a marsh.

Bakwerner turned vermilion and stuttered. He found his tongue. "My lord, it is a lie someone has told you. I never did him harm. We fought, but Hormin fought with many. We've all heard someone killed him, but none of us has left the records all morning. I'm innocent—we're all innocent."

"You tried to strangle Hormin three days ago," Meren said. He rolled the papyrus roll shut and studied Bakwerner. "I am not a judge or a governor. I don't listen to petitions or excuses. Loosen your tongue unless you'd rather sing to the accompaniment of the whip or the stave."

Bakwerner fell to his knees and babbled. "Have pity, excellent lord. I am innocent. It's true that Hormin and I exchanged blows, but you don't know what he did. Three days ago I put the records for the taxes of the city of Busiris on a shelf belonging to Hormin. It was a mistake, my lord, an innocent mistake. But Hormin threw the records away in my absence. The whole of the taxes of Busiris. Gone. He said he didn't look at them, that they didn't belong in his shelf, so he threw them away."

"So you killed him."

"No! No, my lord. That is, I became possessed. He did it deliberately because he was jealous. He knew I was the better scribe. No, my lord, after we fought, I was drained of the fiend that possessed me, and I never touched Hormin again."

"Then if you didn't kill the man, tell me what you know of those more capable of murder."

Bakwerner sat back on his heels. His glance slid from the hem of Meren's kilt to the floor bedside him. "My lord, no one had more cause to desire Hormin's death than his own family. Look to the wife and sons of Hormin."

"Yes?"

"Hormin was a man risen from the people, the son of a butcher who caught the eye of a scribe of the fields. He rose to a great height for so humble a man, yet he kept his wife instead of putting her aside and taking a woman of breeding. But Hormin kept his wife plainly, without costly jewels or robes, and he doled out little of his possessions to the sons, though they are grown." Bakwerner swallowed and lowered his voice. "And he was jealous of his own son. Djaper feeds upon knowledge the way a crocodile feeds on fish. The lad is twenty, but he already knows far more than Hormin did at twice the age."

Meren walked around Bakwerner until he was directly behind him. He let the man sit on the floor waiting for him to speak. Bakwerner wiped beads of sweat from his upper lip.

"Where were you during the night, Bakwerner?"

The scribe almost turned his head, but stopped himself in time. "At home, my lord."

Meren turned quietly away from the office of records and tithes, leaving Bakwerner sitting on the floor in front of the shelves. Once outside, he set out in the direction of the house of the dead scribe along with the two charioteers who were his protection and his shadows. He liked walking. It gave him a chance to think without risking interruption from servants or courtiers.

Ahmose had said that Bakwerner was a physical coward. It was rare for Meren to beat someone he suspected of a crime, though such methods were usual among the city police and other officials of the king. Having been the victim of such methods, he was convinced that if one asked questions with a whip, one only got the answers one wanted to hear, not necessarily the truth. The whip could be used later, if needed, after he flushed a few more birds out of their nests in the papyrus swamp.

The problem was, as Master Ahmose had assured him, that he would have trouble finding anyone who knew Hormin who did not want to kill the man.

His task was to discover who had wanted to kill Hormin enough to risk doing evil in the Place of Anubis.

3

Meren could hear the wails and screams before he reached the street where Hormin had lived. Word of the scribe's death had reached his family, and someone had already hired professional mourners to ply their trade on the small loggia that protected the entrance to the house. One tore at her hair. Another beat her breasts and moaned. The third shrieked on such a high note that Meren covered his ears. His two assistants did the same.

He had seen better performances. Whoever hired the mourners had not paid enough to get the extras. No raking of nails on flesh, no throwing of earth over the body. Meren hurried by the women, only to encounter the household porter. The man bowed several times, but Meren gave him no chance to protest the intrusion, ordering the porter to conduct him to the family.

Once they were inside, the screams of the mourners faded. The porter led him through an entryway, a columned outer hall, and up a staircase. Meren was halfway up the stairs when a shout made him look up. This was not a wail of grief, but a voice climbing the musical scale in wrath. Like the honking of disturbed geese, voices warred with one another. As Meren gained the second floor he heard a woman yell. It was a sound made powerful by healthy lungs, a noise that filled the world with its clamor.

"Robbery! You picking and sneaking thief. Whore."
A man's voice joined in. "She took the broad collar."

Meren swept by the porter and into the room from
which the noise came. Before him were four people
standing in the midst of a litter of papers, open boxes
and caskets, chairs, and tables. Meren paused inside the
door. One of the women cursed. She picked up something from a table and hurled it at the two men. They
ducked and the missile sped past them to crash at
Meren's feet. It was a faience spice pot. The pottery
cracked and red powder burst forth, spraying Meren's
gold sandals and feet.

The woman who had thrown the pot squeaked and
ducked behind a chair. Meren looked from his sandals
to the woman. She was young, with long arms and legs
strung with tense muscles and a short, sharp nose like
the beak of a sparrow.

Knowing that he had startled them all, Meren
directed his gaze to each of the quarrelers. The older
woman was looking at him with a puzzled expression.
She had the dark brown skin of a peasant but the
uncallused hands of a lady. Standing in front of her was
a man as tall as she was, who had not made a sound
when the others were shouting at the young woman.
Beside him was a shorter man, a youth really. He bal-
anced on the balls of his feet and caressed one of his
wrists with his hand. Twisting the wrist back and forth
within the grasp of his fingers, he stared at Meren.

They were trying to decide who he might be. It was
a favorite tactic of his to appear without announcement,
to disturb and unbalance. He knew they were taking in
the transparent robe that fell to his ankles and covered
a kilt belted in red and gold. His long court wig and inlaid dagger would cause apprehension, as would the
two men who stood behind him like bodyguards, for

only a great man walks abroad in fine linen, carries a warrior's blade, and commands charioteers.

"I am Meren." The name caused a stirring among them like papyrus reeds shifting in the north wind. Four heads lowered, and Meren received their bows. "Evil has been done in the sacred place of embalming, and I am sent to hunt out the criminal who murdered the scribe Hormin."

Lifting his foot out of a hillock of spice, Meren skirted the shards of faience and took a chair of cedar with legs shaped like those of a lion.

"There has been theft in this house?" Meren asked.

Four heads nodded.

"Last night?"

Again the nods.

Meren looked from one bowed head to the other and decided to break up the solid phalanx. If he confronted each of them alone, it would be impossible for them to remain silent.

"I will survey the house and question each of the family." Meren nodded at the older woman. "You, mistress, are the wife of Hormin?"

"Yes, my lord."

This was the voice of the woman who had yelled as he came upstairs.

"Take your family to the dining hall and await my summons." It was his experience that the anxiety of waiting to be examined by one of the Eyes and Ears of Pharaoh loosened tongues.

One of his men ushered the family out and went with them. When they were gone Meren summoned the porter, who produced the chief manservant. With this guide and his remaining assistant, Meren toured the house of Hormin.

It was the house of a prosperous scribe; there were

many such in the capital of the empire. A basement housed workrooms used for weaving, bread making, and other chores. Above lay a reception hall and dining room, and above these the family bedrooms and lavatory. On the roof was the kitchen.

To Meren the house appeared ordinary. White-plastered, painted with friezes of lotus petals and geometric designs in bright red, blue, yellow, and green, it contained simple furnishings. The beds, tables, stools, and chairs were of good but not costly wood, the seats of woven rushes.

On the way back from his tour, Meren stuck his head in the door of the scribe's bedchamber. The bed sat at the far end; clothing boxes and a cosmetic table were arranged around the walls. One of his men knelt at a box that held Hormin's kilts, lifted each one, and laid it on the floor.

Meren turned away and headed for the room where he'd first encountered Hormin's family, the man's personal office. Here the furniture was of cedar inlaid with ebony and ivory. Gilt paint adorned Hormin's chair and table, and there were three boxes and four storage caskets, each of expensive wood. One was inlaid with ivory and ebony marquetry. Several alabaster lamps rested on tables, and there was one casket carved from the same stone.

All of the containers bore Hormin's name. Meren touched the obsidian knob on the lid of the alabaster casket, lifted the cover, and placed it aside. Within were fourteen glass bottles and vials. Meren unstopped a vial and sniffed the perfume within. He opened a pot and touched the tip of his finger to the salve within. It was unguent; from the scent, costly unguent, made of foreign spices and resins. Yet it wasn't the same as that he'd found on Hormin's kilt.

Replacing the unguent, Meren summoned the porter

and ordered him to bring the wife of Hormin to him. He arranged himself in Hormin's chair and picked up a gilt penholder from the table beside him. Removing the top, he shook out several reed pens and replaced them. He was twirling the penholder when the porter announced Selket, the wife of Hormin.

She must have been of an age with her husband, for Selket bore the signs of middle age. There were pockets of flesh beneath her eyes. The flesh of her upper arms drooped like empty barley sacks, and her skin was as cracked and dry as old wood left in the desert. Without speaking to her, Meren knew that this woman had spent her youth laboring in the sun and heat. She stood before him with her eyes fixed on sheets of papyrus scattered on the floor at her feet. Meren gave her permission to sit, and the woman took a stool.

"Please accept my condolences upon the death of your husband, mistress. I'm here to seek out his murderer."

Selket's face had been as blank as the outfacing wall of a house. At his words, it cracked open and from it erupted a flood of venom.

"It's her. She killed him for his wealth or to hide her depravities. She beds any pretty man who comes into her sight, you know. My husband must have found her out." Selket's arms swept around indicating the disturbed room. "Or perhaps she killed him for finding her in his office pilfering."

"Who?"

"Beltis, my lord. That creature who tried to wound you with the spice pot. She is my—was my husband's concubine."

This was why Meren cultivated the skill of listening. He remembered the admonition of the sage Ptahhotep, which advised a wise man not to listen to the spouting of the hot-bellied. He had found that listening to the hot-bellied often led to the discovery of the truth.

Meren set the penholder back on the table and regarded Selket. "You're telling me that you know the girl killed your husband? You will go before the royal magistrates and give testimony?"

Selket started to speak, then closed her mouth. Her lips pinched together and she shook her head. Meren lifted a brow, but made no comment. She was unwilling to risk the punishment for bearing false witness, but her reticence might not signal an untruth. After all, she could be beaten and starved for three days, or even put to death, for perjury.

"What was the course of your husband's last day?" Meren asked.

"It was like most days," Selket said. "He rose. From her bed. And he ate his morning meal here. Then she came in while I was serving him, and demanded some trinket." Each time Selket referred to the concubine, she hissed out the word "she" as though it tasted of dung. "She is always complaining that she has no jewelry, not enough shifts or wigs or cosmetics."

As he listened to Selket, Meren became aware of his own vague uneasiness. At first he couldn't understand his discomfort, but then he realized that the woman talking to him shifted from fury to complacency and back again in half a heartbeat. When she spoke of Beltis, her eyes took on the look of a rabid hyena, yet moments before she'd mentioned Hormin with a sweet lilt in her voice.

"And after he dined, your husband went to the office of records and tithes," Meren said. "He spoke to no one else before he left?"

Selket had been breathing rapidly from the force of her ire. Suddenly she smiled. "Only to me, about the house, and about our sons. They were avoiding him because he was still a bit angry with them. Imsety, my oldest, wanted the old farm since Hormin dislikes husbandry. Djaper supported Imsety, but Hormin wouldn't give it up. It gives us a prosperous living with Hormin's wages. Imsety would have still handed over the proper share to his father, but Hormin was furious at the idea." Selket waved a hand. "Sons and fathers will contend, no matter a mother's wishes."

Meren got up, motioning for Selket to remain where she was. He stooped and picked up a sheaf of papers, household accounts.

"Go on, mistress."

"My husband went to the office of records and tithes and returned at midday. He ate and went to her, but they fought again. I could hear her shouting at him even though they were in her room. She wanted Hormin to give her a set of bracelets, and he wouldn't."

Selket laughed, and Meren winced at the loud, barking sound.

"I heard him slap her, then he left and didn't return until afternoon. After he was gone, Beltis ran away."

Meren cocked his head to the side. The heavy strands of his wig swung to his shoulder, and he nodded for her to continue.

Selket sniffed. "She runs away all the time. To her parents in the tomb-makers' village on the west bank. Hormin always fetches her back. He did yesterday, unfortunately. When they returned, we all dined." Selket paused and contemplated her brown hands. "My husband spent the rest of the evening with her, and I know nothing of what they did. When I rose this morning, I didn't know he was gone from the house until Djaper couldn't find him. It was while we were looking for my husband that we found his office wrecked and looted.

Later, a priest came from the Place of Anubis and told me that he was dead."

Selket pressed her lips together, and Meren was surprised to see a tear creep out of the corner of one eye. He would never understand some women. She mourned Hormin; he would have been tempted to put the man in his house of eternity long ago.

"And your sons," Meren said. "You say they quarreled with their father."

The flow of tears dammed up at once, and Selket shook her head. "Only a little. They are dutiful sons. Imsety takes care of the farm outside the city. He only came to ask about getting the deed put in his name, and he'll have to go back soon, to oversee the harvest. Djaper follows the path of his father, and I hope he'll take Hormin's place at the office of records and tithes."

Meren shuffled the papyrus sheets in his hands. Taking his seat again, he laid the papers on the table nearby. One of his assistants would question the servants so that stories about the family's movements could be confirmed. He expected everyone to claim to have slept through the night, for unless one were privileged, work was hot and long. The day began with first light and ended with nightfall.

Tapping his fingers on the arm of his chair, Meren contemplated the furrows between Selket's brow. The woman was little more than a housekeeper to her husband. Her resentment bubbled on the surface like molten copper in a smith's crucible. The two women worried over Hormin, two jackals fighting over a carcass. Hormin had been enamored of the concubine Beltis, yet he hadn't set aside his wife. Why?

"Mistress," Meren said. "Your husband was the son of a butcher who attained the honored position of scribe. You must have been proud."

Selket's weather-roughened features relaxed, and Meren caught a glimpse of a young woman whose eyes were bright with pride and whose face wasn't parched from the heat of resentment.

"He worked so hard, and he was so careful to attend to the officials who could place him well. When he was given the position of scribe of records and tithes, we held a feast." Selket's smile turned into a frown. "But the seasons went by with no other advancement. Hormin saw others less talented but more capable of flattery raised above him. Only a few weeks ago he learned that Bakwerner would be set above him."

In spite of his much-practiced control, Meren started when Selket's voice rose abruptly and she beat one fist into her palm with a force that would leave a bruise.

Clasping her hands together, Selket leaned toward Meren. "My lord, Hormin was an unhappy man. He told me that Bakwerner was jealous because he knew that Hormin was a better scribe." As she went on, Selket's voice got louder. "It was unfair that my husband wasn't preferred. He waited for so long. Why, if he had been given his due, he would never have taken Beltis. What is she but a burden?"

"A burden?" Meren asked. Selket gave her head a little shake and appeared to remember with whom she was talking. She quieted.

"She is lazy, my lord. She does no chores. She doesn't help with the cooking. All she does is tend to herself. She bathes and arranges her hair and puts on lotions and ointments and cosmetics. And then she goes to the courtyard and lies in the shade or walks to the market to purchase trinkets for herself." Selket lowered her voice. "And she opens her legs for other men. She is a fiend; she doesn't even tend to her little son. Hormin purchased a slave girl to do that."

Meren rose and went to an alcove that held a statue of the god Toth, patron of scribes. He contemplated the man's body and ibis head while he waited for Selket to continue. When she remained silent, he glanced back at her. She was chewing on her lip and eyeing him. He'd seen that look of apprehension before in those who suspect that they have said more than they should.

"Beltis wanted to supplant you?" Meren said this while he resumed his stroll about the room. Avoiding the scattered contents of a jewel box, he stopped to run his fingertips over the lid of a casket.

"But my lord," Selket said. She smiled with the open grimace of a monkey. "Beltis never understood Hormin as I did. If she had, she would have known he would never divorce me. Our marriage agreement provides for a generous settlement for me if we part. Hormin and I, we know what it is to work, and to need. We don't give up what is ours."

Contemplating Selket's expression of pleasure, Meren nodded. "One thing more. When I arrived you were all fighting about a robbery. You say someone has taken objects from this room. What is missing?"

"I'm not sure. Hormin never allowed anyone in here by themselves, and he kept the valuables under his own hand. Djaper says he saw his father place a broad collar in that casket." Selket pointed to an ebony and ivory container. "He said it had beads of gold, lapis lazuli, and red jasper. I've never seen it, but then, Djaper often worked here with his father, and the piece was new. He promised it to her."

Selket glanced around the room. "There is an inventory somewhere. Djaper also says there are copper ingots missing. She probably stole them."

Meren turned around to face Selket. She was angry at the loss of such rich pieces, but there was no sign of apprehension, or awareness that it was odd that Hormin owned a necklace of gold and precious stones and hadn't given it to her. It was as if she were long used to her husband's miserliness. Perhaps she was. In any case, he couldn't believe she didn't covet such a beautiful piece of jewelry as the missing broad collar.

He was about to dismiss Selket when a crash made the woman jump. He was out of the room and bounding down the stairs before Selket got to her feet. Meren rounded the corner of the dining hall in time to dodge a ceramic lamp that sailed past his head and crashed against a wall.

Barely missing the wooden lampstand, Meren rushed into the hall to see the concubine Beltis lift a wine jar from its pedestal and hurl it at her younger brother-in-law. Djaper was bending over Imsety, who was curled up on the floor nursing his groin. Meren shouted at him, and he ducked. The wine jar bounced off Djaper's shoulder and hit the ground. Pottery cracked, and wine sloshed over the groaning Imsety.

Meren ran to Beltis and caught her before she could lift a stone vase from a table. Knocking the vase aside, he grabbed the woman by the waist and lifted her off her feet. Beltis let out a scream. She kicked backward, catching Meren on the shin.

"Abomination." Meren grunted under the impact of an elbow to his ribs.

"Dung eater!" Beltis screamed at Djaper. "Lover of boys, I curse your *ka*."

Djaper sprang at Beltis. Meren saw him make a fist and draw back his arm. Swinging so that Djaper missed Beltis, he blocked the punch with his free arm. It was a blow of the force one used only on another man. Djaper fell back as soon as his arm touched Meren.

Beltis was still shouting curses at her brothers-in-law

while she clawed at Meren's arms. Losing what patience was left to him, Meren hoisted the woman on his hip. When she tried to bite his thigh, he shifted her weight to both arms and threw her to the ground. Beltis landed on her buttocks with a howl and looked up for the first time. Panting, she brushed aside strands of her wig and caught sight of Meren. The panting stopped. Her eyelids climbed high and disappeared. Beltis whimpered and began to crawl toward Meren.

In no mood for groveling, Meren halted the concubine with one word. He looked around and spotted a charioteer near Djaper and Imsety. The man was on the floor nursing a cut above his eye. In the doorways of the hall servants hovered, uncertain and curious.

Surveying the wreckage, Meren beckoned to the porter. "Put the woman in her room and see that she doesn't leave it."

"Lord, her *ka* is inhabited by fiends," Djaper said.

Meren straightened the folds of his robe. "What happened?"

"I told her to go back to her parents' house. We don't want her here."

Meren surveyed the face of Hormin's youngest son. Clean-shaven, with small features, it was the face of a youth on the body of a man in his breeding years. Djaper met his gaze openly, and Meren was sure that he was meant to see the ingenuous candor of a boy.

"You may both retire to your rooms."

The men bowed to him, and Meren was left to the ministrations of the household servants. A maid offered cool water and beer. Another brought moist towels and salve for the cuts on his arms. The furrows weren't deep, but they stung. Meren tended to them himself, downed a cup of beer, and headed for the room occupied by the woman called Beltis.

She was waiting for him. Meren was surprised at how quickly she had recovered from the battle and shock of having lifted her hand to him. She was wearing a fresh shift, a costly one of transparent drapes and folds that fastened below her breasts.

Meren stalked into the chamber and seated himself in an armchair. Beltis walked toward him, and he realized that she had oiled and rouged her bare breasts and lips and applied fresh eye paint. She held her arms to her sides, but she pressed them inward so that her breasts pointed forward and the nipples danced as she moved.

He almost laughed. He would have, but Beltis reached him, dropped to her knees, and flung her arms about his legs. She began whispering abject regrets. Slick flesh pressed against his legs, and her hand fastened on his bare ankle. It slid up his calf. Fingers reached his inner thigh, and Meren caught them.

"Remove yourself from me."

Beltis sat back on her heels and clasped her hands in her lap. Meren noticed that she still held her arms close to her breasts. Her chest heaved, and to his surprise, she appeared unable to lift her eyes from his legs. No, they had moved. By the gods, the woman was staring at his groin.

It had been many seasons since he'd been shocked by a woman. He was shocked by this one. Her tongue laved her lips as once more she studied the brown flesh of his thigh visible through his robe. Suddenly Beltis bent low. Meren felt moist lips on the top of his foot. Hot breath tickled his skin as she whispered to him.

"Forgive me, great lord. I was driven to madness by those cruel men, and now I behold the virility of a lion, such beauty."

"Get up," Meren said. Beltis raised her head. Her lips were slack. He supposed their open readiness had brought rewards before. "I said get up. One would think the death of a generous master would have you weeping with the mourners outside."

Beltis sat up and regarded him as a scribe regards a schoolboy. "Great lord, I served my master according to a contract freely made. If you could speak to him, he would tell you how I pleased him. But the master was cursed with an ungrateful, selfish wife and sons. They are his family, but they don't grieve. Do they abstain from meat and wine? Do Djaper and Imsety fail to cut their hair and beards? Selket still bathes and paints her face. And none of them have gone to Hormin's mortuary chapel to weep for him."

"I'm not interested in weeping. I'm interested in what Hormin did on the night he was killed. Mistress Selket says he spent the night with you."

"Indeed." Beltis smirked at him. "Hormin craved me as a bull lusts after his cows. I gave him much pleasure, with my hands and—"

Meren spoke with deliberate slowness and clearly pronounced words. "When did Hormin leave your bed?"

"I don't know, my lord." Beltis sighed and lifted her shoulders. "I was exhausted from our play and slept heavily. I woke after the sun was up, and the master was gone."

"He told you nothing of where he might go?"

Shaking her head, Beltis cast her eyes down. "I am only a concubine."

"Yes." Meren rose and went to stand behind the chair. "So you heard nothing during the night, even though your master's office isn't far from this room."

Beltis's head shot up. "I didn't need to hear anything. I know one of them robbed my master. They were taking his possessions, and he caught them." The concubine narrowed her eyes. "They fought with my master, lord. Those two sons wanted his farm all to themselves. I heard them yelling at each other."

"How is it that you heard what must have been a private talk?"

"I listened at the door, Lord Meren. I have to protect my son, and you can see why after what happened today. And now they want to blame me for all the evil. They hate me, Selket and Imsety and Djaper. They would like to see me condemned for his death. If he'd lived, Hormin would have given me more of his wealth, and entered my son in his will."

"You witness against all three. Yet you say you slept the night." Meren traced the carving on the back of the chair and waited.

Beltis pursed her lips. "My slave girl, she says the brothers went out after the evening meal and didn't return until almost morning. If my poor lord was killed in the Place of Anubis, they could have set upon him."

"All the servants will be questioned," Meren said. "I'll find out where each of you was during the night. Each of you." When Beltis appeared undisturbed, Meren continued. "You were screaming about a necklace being taken when I found you all in Hormin's office."

"Yes, lord, I tell you Djaper took it, or Imsety, or Selket. They all hated it that the master bestowed gifts upon me. This was a broad collar of great beauty and cost. It was of gold and lapis lazuli and red jasper." Beltis chewed on her lower lip and scowled. "The master promised it to me, but it's gone."

Meren said nothing. His men would take inventory of Hormin's possessions and question the household to confirm the family's claims. He resumed his seat, taking care to move the chair so that he was too far away from Beltis for her to pounce on him again. Having basked in the favor of ladies far more sophisticated, intelligent, and lovely than Beltis, he had no desire to be mauled.

"You fought with your master," he said. "On the day of his death you quarreled with him and ran away to the tomb-makers' village on the west bank."

Soft laughter bubbled up at him, and Beltis laid her head to one side. "A quarrel between lovers, my lord. We had many, and always my master begged me to forgive him. He needed me. Why, if he had to do without me for even one night, he was as engorged as a stud ox."

"Spare me your stories of Hormin's lust. What was the quarrel about?"

"I wanted matching bracelets for my new broad collar, and he wouldn't have them made." Beltis tossed her head. "I am a woman of great beauty, and I deserve jewels and fine robes. Hormin made me so angry. He could have given me twenty bracelets if he weren't so greedy. I was angry, so I went away. After all, he is— was so much more generous after a few nights without me."

Meren began to think that Hormin was not only a hot-bellied man, but a fool as well.

"You see, lord, my father is a sculptor in the tomb-makers' village, so it is not far for me to go. I went there yesterday after Hormin slapped me, and I waited for him to come for me. He did, and we made up our quarrel. He even took me to see his tomb before we left. It's on the edge of the nobles' cemetery. Then we came home."

"And during all the time you were together, Hormin never spoke of going to the Place of Anubis, or of anyone who had threatened him?"

"No, great lord." Beltis raised her voice. "But I'm sure that Selket has accused me. She hates me for being beautiful while she is ugly and old. The brothers are the same. Imsety is stupid, and Djaper hates me."

The concubine's rancor swelled as she related her trials. "They will all tell you lies about me, but I'll tell you the truth. Djaper hates me because I spurned him when he would have lain with me and because my son displaced him in the heart of Hormin. I tell you they killed my master so that my son and I wouldn't take their place in his will."

"Enough."

Meren shoved himself out of his chair. He took Beltis's hand and helped her rise. As soon as she was up, he dropped her hand and went to the door. While he was opening it, he spoke again.

"While he was with you, did Hormin spill perfume on himself?"

Beltis furrowed her brow. "No, my lord."

Meren stepped out of the bedchamber. He looked back at Beltis, and saw that she had resumed her posture with her breasts pressed forward. Determination seemed to be a great part of her character. Meren surveyed the gleaming nipples, then let his eyes slowly drift to Beltis's face.

"You say the wife and sons of Hormin are guilty of this murder. Over and over you have complained that they hate you. If they hate you so, Beltis, tell me why it wasn't you who was found buried in natron with a blade stuck in your pretty neck?"

4

After a few hours he'd grown used to the stench of the Place of Anubis, but it would take an eternity of the gods to accustom himself to the priest Raneb's screeching. Kysen tried not to wince as Raneb flapped his bony arms and cawed at a hapless apprentice who was unlucky enough not to know anything about Hormin, his life, or his death. The priest raised an arm, and Kysen sucked in his breath. He turned away and pretended to study one of the natron tables. The old miasma engulfed him, and he was a child again, bewildered and cowering under blows he was sure would kill him.

That clenched fist, the swinging arm, they belonged to Raneb, who would hurt no one. When he turned back to the group of men in the drying shed, he was calm. From the fire stokers to the highest priest, all had been questioned either by Kysen or one of his men. Further haranguing would yield nothing.

"Priest Raneb."

Raneb shut his mouth in midscreech.

"Many thanks for your priceless assistance. The justice of Pharaoh is greatly aided by the authority of one such as you."

It had taken him years to learn the use of flattery, to learn how to spy out one susceptible to it, to say ridiculous phrases as though they were as weighty as sacred chants from *The Book of the Dead*. Meren had taught him. The greatest difficulty lay in believing his father when he said that the receiver of the flattery wouldn't see through to its real purpose. To Kysen the end was transparent.

Chest puffed with self-importance, nose and cheeks red, the priest glanced about to assure himself that everyone had heard the words of the son of Lord Meren. Rocking back and forth, toe to heel, he folded his hands over his belly and asked what else he could do.

"At the moment, little." Kysen shook his head in regret. "Much as I wish to remain, duty calls me away. But I would speak once more with the water carrier."

The servant was brought forth, the others dismissed. Getting rid of Raneb was more difficult, but Kysen accomplished this task and set about the chore of allaying the fears of a peasant faced with a great lord. He couldn't do much about the charioteer's bronze corselet strapped across his chest, the warrior's wristguards, the weapons at his waist. The youth was one of the thousands of children of the poor who served in menial capacities in the temples, palaces, and households of the Two Lands. He would fear Kysen because he was common, landless, and of no importance to anyone but himself.

"Sit up, boy. I can't talk to you if your nose is in the dirt."

The youth raised his upper body, but kept his eyes downcast as was proper. He wasn't much younger than Kysen. His face was wide from forehead to chin. He was short, and thin from too little food and too much work. His bottom lip had been chewed raw in the time since Kysen had last seen him. It wasn't surprising, since the poor water carrier was the only one at the Place of Anubis who had recognized Hormin.

"Your name is Sedi?"

Sedi's nose burrowed into the dirt again.

"Don't do that!" Kysen bit back a curse as Sedi's body went stiff and then trembled. "By the phallus of Ra, they've been filling your head with silly tales of being carried off to a cell and beaten. Well, you can cast such fear from your heart. I don't beat innocent children."

Sedi's mouth opened in astonishment, and Kysen grinned at him. He lapsed into the slang of his childhood.

"Steady your skiff, brother."

"Oh."

Kysen dropped to one knee beside Sedi. "Oh? You sound like a washer maid whose lover has thrown her down among the reeds at the riverbank. Surely you heard my origin in my speech." Kysen held out his right hand, palm up. "Do you think I got these scars from such light work as hefting a sword? And stop chewing your lip. It's bleeding."

"Yes, lord."

"You may speak freely to me. I give you permission, Sedi."

"I did nothing! There was a crowd around the body, and I came to look. It's not my fault. I did nothing."

Kysen put a hand on Sedi's shoulder, and the youth jumped.

"I asked you to speak freely, but I do expect you to make sense. You're beginning to sound like Raneb."

Sedi made a choking sound and then lost the battle not to laugh. Through the hand that rested on the water carrier's shoulder, Kysen could feel tense muscles relax.

"Brother, don't you think I know the courage it took for you to come forward with your knowledge? Everyone knows it's best to leave the affairs of the great alone. If you speak before great men you are as a reed before pylons, no?"

"Yes, lord." Sedi wet his lips and swallowed. "But Raneb has been good to me, and I couldn't let evil flourish in the Place of Anubis."

Kysen eased his body down to sit beside Sedi, and eased into his question as well. "Then you understand that it's important for me to know how you recognized Hormin."

"I've seen him perhaps three times."

"Here?"

"No, lord, in the village of the tomb makers of Pharaoh."

Kysen felt the strength drain from his arms and legs, and he was glad that he was sitting down. "Tell me."

"We came to Thebes last Drought in search of work and found it at the tomb-makers' village. My father is servant to the painter Useramun. Raneb has allowed me to visit him on feast days, and I saw Hormin there. I think he was paying the servants of the Great Place to decorate his tomb. You know they take on extra work to be done after their service to Pharaoh is done each day."

"I know," Kysen said. "So you've only been at the village a short time. How often did Hormin go there?"

"I don't know, Lord Kysen. I only saw him briefly, and by chance."

"What was he doing?"

"Once he was yelling at the chief scribe, once he was yelling at a draftsman, and another time he was walking down the path to the landing at the river."

"Hormin yelled a lot."

Sedi nodded.

"But you know nothing else of his business at the village?"

"No, Lord Kysen. I am but a water carrier, son of a humble cup bearer, but . . ."

Kysen watched Sedi chew on his lip. "You won't suffer for your honesty."

"I don't think anyone in the tomb-makers' village liked Hormin."

"How do you know?"

"I'm not sure, lord." Sedi squinted and stared out into the white heat of the afternoon. "I think it came to me because whenever I saw Hormin, I noticed that everyone else seemed anxious to find something to do elsewhere. He must have been an unpleasant man."

Kysen smiled. "Someone found him unpleasant indeed. You've done well, Sedi."

Rising to his feet, Kysen motioned for Sedi to get up. Over the youth's shoulder he saw the approach of his men. They'd finished their examination of the Place of Anubis. He glanced at Sedi, and found the water carrier watching him anxiously. Kysen knew what it meant to feel helpless in the face of happenings one didn't understand. Before his men came within hearing distance Kysen whispered to the youth, "If you remember something else, come to the house of my father in the Street of the Falcon near the palace. And listen, brother. Should you need help, or if you lose place because of this evil, come to me."

This time Kysen didn't object when Sedi fell to his knees. When his men reached them, he had assumed the proper attitude of a lord receiving the obeisance of an inferior. Without looking at the water carrier on the ground beside him, Kysen walked out of the drying shed and stepped into his chariot.

On the way back to the palace district he tried not to think of the possibility that he would have to go to the tomb-makers' village. He hadn't been back there since his real father had dragged him from it ten years ago. The village lay a short distance north and west of the offices of the government of Pharaoh, yet Kysen managed never to see it even if he happened to look in that direction. The good god Amun had given him new life on the day his father sold him to Meren. The old life was as dead as the ancient ones in their pyramids.

As he approached the great walled house that had sheltered the count's family for generations, Kysen's spirit lifted. Perhaps Remi would be awake from his nap. Leaving his team in the hands of a groom, he forsook the ovenlike day for the darkness of the entryway. The difference in temperature was so great that he shivered. A maid came forward with cool water to drink and wet cloths to bathe his face, hands, and feet.

Kysen was bending over to slip on a sandal when he heard the clatter of metal wheels. A miniature bronze chariot raced across the tiled floor. Kysen snatched up his sandal and hopped over the vehicle before it rammed his toes.

"Father, I slay you!"

Small feet planted apart, body turned sideways in imitation of an archer's stance, Remi let fly a blunt-tipped arrow that hit the floor in front of Kysen. Kysen groaned, clutched his chest, and crumpled to the floor on his back. Remi gave a loud whoop and flew at his father. A three-year-old sandbag landed on his chest, making Kysen grunt.

"Sweetmeats, Father. Nurse won't give me sweetmeats. You give them to me."

"I can't," Kysen said with his eyes closed. "I'm dead."

Remi bounced on his father's chest with each of his words. "No, you're not. I unkill you. Now the sweetmeats."

From the courtyard a shrill voice with the force of a hyena's call said Remi's name, and Kysen's eyes popped open. He groaned.

"Why didn't you tell me your mother had come to visit?"

Remi scooted off his father and dived for his toy chariot. "I forgot."

"Kysen, what are you doing?"

Rolling over on his stomach, Kysen rested his forehead on the cold tile. "I'm dead. Remi killed me."

"Nonsense. Quit wallowing on the floor."

Kysen turned his head and looked at the woman in the doorway. She was still lovely in spite of her indulgence in wine and potions mixed by her magician priests. She had the largest eyes and widest lips of any woman he'd ever met, and she was dressed as usual in a complicated court robe, gold and carnelian broad collar, and long wig. Her oiled lips were twisted in distaste.

"Has it been a month already, Taweret?"

"You know it has, and Remi and I have been playing."

"You? You and Remi have been playing?" Kysen propped himself up on his forearms and stared at his former wife. Behind him Remi trundled his chariot around in a circle.

"Mother watches me shoot Nurse."

"You should include your mother in the game, Remi. Shoot her."

Remi stopped pushing his chariot and looked around for his bow and arrow.

"I will not be shot," Taweret said. She clasped her hands together in front of her body, straightened her shoulders, and turned on her heel.

Kysen sighed and got up to follow her. She'd come to look at her tainted son and his low father, to remind herself once again of her misfortune and the wisdom of her divorce. He'd stand her presence as long as he could and then take refuge in the workshop where the physician would be examining Hormin's body. Once again he thanked the good god that he'd never really loved Taweret.

She had stretched out on a couch under a stand of palms in the courtyard. Two of her servants fanned her with ostrich-feather fans. She watched him come toward her, eyeing him with that critical wariness that never left her when he was present.

Kysen dropped down to sit by the edge of the artificial pool. He scooped water into his hand and drank, and was rewarded with a sneer at his common behavior. He considered shedding his armor and kilt to bathe in the pool, but he didn't want to lengthen Taweret's visit.

"Only peasants drink from their hands."

Kysen let a handful of water dribble down his bent knee to his ankle. "Some are born to be peasants. Some the gods ordain to become beer brewers, goldsmiths, architects. Do you know what the gods made you, Taweret? A sufferer. That's why you married me. So you could suffer. Was it worth it, that exquisite pain and the virtue of bearing it?" Kysen smiled at his wife's glare. "Obviously not, or you wouldn't have divorced me."

"I am *henemmet*—"

"I know. Your mother's father's mother's mother was the spawn of a harem woman and Pharaoh. A thin strain of divinity, it seems to me. Though once I was willing to kneel before you for it. But then my knees got sore, and I decided I had enough gods and goddesses to worship, and that one living god was enough for me."

Taweret jumped off the couch, sending cushions flying. She picked one up and threw it at Kysen on her way out.

"I was right to divorce you! You're lower than a dog's belly. All my friends say so. All of them, do you hear?" Taweret's voice rose as she got farther away, and then cut off when she neared the approach to the street. The fan bearers scurried after her.

Kysen heard a door slam, and Remi appeared, chariot dragging along behind him by a length of twine.

"She's gone," he said with a smile. "Now may I have a sweetmeat?"

Pleased with himself for having got rid of Taweret so easily, Kysen picked up a pillow and went to the couch.

"You may have two sweetmeats. Tell Nurse I gave permission." As Remi pattered away, Kysen went on. "And remember what happened the last time you lied and told her I said you could have five."

Fluffing the pillows in his hands, Kysen lay on his back and stuffed the cushion beneath his head. He stared up through the palm leaves at the sky. Soon the servants would bring food. They always knew when he was ready to dine; he'd yet to figure out how.

The physician attached to his father's staff would have Hormin's body by now. Great care would be taken to ascertain if magic had been used to cause the man's death. Kysen didn't expect to find such signs of tampering. He'd been assisting his father since he was a youth, and what Meren had told him from the beginning was true. Those who employed magic almost always helped the supernatural along by use of ordinary weapons, poisons, or other violence. He was contemplating what the physician would have to say about Hormin's body when someone began chanting over him. Something hit his ear, and Kysen yelped. He scrambled to his feet to face his son's nurse.

"I adjure thee," Mutemwia said, "by the holy names, render up the murderer who has carried away this Hormin—Khalkhak, Khalkoum, Khiam, Khar, Khroum, Zbar, Beri, Zbarkom—and by the terrible names—Balltek, Apep, Seba."

Kysen rubbed his ear and cursed the girl. She reached out with a small wooden hammer and tapped him on the other ear. Yowling, Kysen scuttled backward.

"Render up the murderer who has carried off this Hormin. As long as I strike the ear with this hammer, let the eye of the murderer be smitten and inflamed until it betrays him."

Nurse lifted the hammer again, but Kysen snatched it from her hand.

"By the phallus of Ra! Are you mad?" Kysen threw the little hammer into the pond and rounded on the girl. His ears stung, and now his head hurt as well. "Hathor gave you much beauty and no wits."

Nurse Mutemwia crossed her arms over her chest and scowled at Kysen. "It is a spell to protect you and find the evil one, lord. Do you wear your Eye of Horus amulet?"

"Beaten by my son's nurse. Curse you, Mutemwia, I don't care if your family has served Meren's for generations, you shouldn't hit my ears." Kysen rubbed the injured organs. "Did you break the skin?"

Mutemwia shook her head. A clap of her hands summoned servants bearing food. "This servant humbly begs pardon. She only has thy welfare before her eyes."

Kysen cast a suspicious glance at the girl. When Mutemwia was humble, he grew wary.

"Nebamun is the physician and priest in this household. There's no need for you to do his work for him."

"I got the spell from him," Mutemwia said as she set a table before the couch. She dismissed the servants and began dishing out roast oryx. "I practiced the words of power while Lady Taweret was here."

"Ha!"

Mutemwia ignored Kysen and poured wine into a goblet, her expression as calm as it had been since she entered the courtyard.

"You're jealous," Kysen said.

"A humble nurse is too far below a descendant of a living god to dare to be jealous of her."

Kysen scowled at her again, sent pillows flying from the couch with a swipe of his arm, and sat down. He bit into a joint of oryx. He chewed and glared at the same time. Bowing, Mutemwia picked up a tray and vanished in the direction of the kitchen. Kysen nearly bit the inside of his cheek, so violent was his chewing. As she vanished, his scowl turned to a grin. He'd have his own revenge tonight.

5

In the house of Hormin, Meren approached the chamber assigned to Djaper. A charioteer stood at the closed door. Meren had left Beltis intent upon examining Hormin's younger son, who'd nearly delivered a mutilating blow to the concubine earlier. He paused beside the charioteer before entering the bedchamber.

"What is he doing, Iry-nufer?"

"Reading, lord."

"Reading?"

Iry-nufer nodded. Meren folded his arms and studied the tip of his sandals. Djaper felt comfortable enough to read in this hour of evil and death.

"The watch has been arranged?" Meren asked.

"Yes, lord."

"One man should be enough. But I want him to stay out of sight. Find a rooftop across the street if you have to."

Meren opened the door a crack and gazed into Djaper's room. The young man was propped up on a couch with a papyrus roll stretched in his hands. He clamped his teeth around a reed pen and frowned at the sheet in front of him. Meren slipped into the room. As he approached, Djaper looked up and released the papyrus roll, which furled into one hand. Removing the pen from his mouth, he dropped it on the scribe's palette on the floor beside him and knelt. The papyrus roll was held at his side behind the folds of his kilt.

Meren inclined his head at Djaper as he walked past the couch to stand in front of a wall lined with shelves. Most were filled with papyrus rolls, old letters, freshly ground ink, sealing clay, and the other accoutrements of a scribe's profession.

Meren returned to the couch and sat down. Djaper was standing with his eyes on the floor in the proper attitude of respect. Meren held out his hand, and Djaper's head jerked up. He slowly held out the roll, waiting in silence as Meren perused it.

"This is an estimate of harvest. I understood that it was your brother who attended to your father's farm."

Djaper's eyes widened, and he smiled. "Yes, Lord Meren. Imsety plants things, plows things, herds things, but sometimes he's too busy to keep all the records. Like now. Harvest is almost upon us."

"What do you know of your father's death?"

Keeping his gaze on his hands, Djaper rolled the papyrus into a smaller tube. "Nothing, lord."

"You fought with him."

"The lord refers to the small argument about Imsety owning the farm." Djaper sighed and let the papyrus roll fall to the floor. "It's true. Father never wanted to give up any of his possessions, but Imsety is the only one who really cares about the farm. Father kept most of the wealth gained by it. Imsety got barely enough to keep himself, and neither of us has enough for a separate household. Father hated farming, and Imsety would have given him whatever share he wanted. So I spoke for my brother two days ago. You see, Imsety can grow anything, but he's no better than a monkey at speaking for himself."

Meren nodded and waved his hand to signal that

Djaper could relax his formal posture. The young man sat back on his heels with his hands folded in his lap.

"All my eloquence went for naught. As I said, Father was furious. I counseled Imsety to wait until after Harvest, to give Father time to get used to the idea. But now—"

"Now you and your brother will inherit."

"Of course, lord. A man's sons care for his eternal house. It is we who will see that prayers are said for his soul, that his *ka* is supplied with meat and drink. It's the proper way. Any dutiful son would do the same."

Meren leaned back and placed his elbow on a pile of pillows. "And what about Beltis?"

An apologetic grin spread across Djaper's face. "I beg forgiveness. The woman attacked poor Imsety, and I couldn't let her hurt him again. You see, lord, Imsety looked after me when I was small and weak. He put up with my tagging along with him, taught me how to shave and throw a dagger. And anyway, that woman has been stealing from us since she came. Last night she got careless and didn't bother to conceal her theft."

"But you didn't see her last night."

"No, my lord. I worked at the office of records and tithes all day, came home to get Imsety, and we spent the whole evening with friends." Djaper bent forward in a confiding manner. "In truth, I was avoiding Father. He was angry with me, and I didn't want to fight again. I left yesterday morning before he did, and spent most of my time in the archives room with two other apprentices. Luckily he went to the temple of Amun on an errand for master Ahmose and then had to chase after Beltis. Last night I made certain that Imsety and I were out until past midnight. I knew that Father would calm down if he didn't have to look at us for a while."

"And you saw nothing of your father last night?"

"Oh no, lord. We dined with a friend. Nu, son of Pen-amun, is his name. And then we all went to the tavern called Eye of Horus for beer and women. A pleasant evening."

Meren rose, and Djaper scrambled to his feet. Strolling about the room, Meren let the silence stretch out. Djaper was entirely too comfortable in his presence, but then, perhaps he was being unfair. Some men did possess a natural composure and openness that enabled them to face difficulties with aplomb. Ay was one. And he himself could face a horde of Nubian bandits smiling—as long as his family was safe.

Meren glanced at Djaper and saw that Hormin's son had risen and was now leaning against his work shelves. One leg was bent, and he'd cocked one foot over the other. He was toying with his wrist again, and Meren gritted his teeth. That mannerism annoyed him; it made him want to rub the brand that marred his own wrist beneath the gold bracelet.

"Hormin was known as a contentious man. It is said that he complained about his lazy, stupid sons to anyone at the office of records and tithes who would listen. Did he chastise you in front of others?"

During Meren's speech Djaper had straightened from his relaxed pose. His face flushed, and he lowered his eyes.

"Father criticized everyone." The words were said quietly, with deliberate lightness, but Djaper's face drained of its crimson hue until it was almost a paste color.

"I wager he criticized you most of all, since you seem to be quite intelligent. From what I understand, your clever heart would be a fly in an open wound to Hormin."

"He was proud of me," Djaper said.

"He said so? You didn't hate him for disgracing you in front of superiors and fellow apprentices?"

Djaper was quiet for a moment before letting a tentative smile pull at his lips. He met Meren's eyes directly, humor making them sparkle.

"The lord is wise, but he forgets that a father can be harsh and yet love his sons. It was so with mine."

"I see. Then you were worried when your father couldn't be found this morning."

"Not at first. We thought he was with Beltis, and she thought he was with us. So it wasn't until the sun was up that we understood that he wasn't in the house at all. I was looking for him when I discovered the theft in his office. And then the priest came and told us he was dead."

"I want a list of the missing possessions," Meren said. He was pacing slowly in front of a table stacked with flat sheets of papyrus. He stopped beside it and glanced at the top sheet. It was a record of taxes from the Hare Nome. "You're diligent in the service of Pharaoh, to work at night."

"It is nothing, lord. The sheet was damaged, and I was copying it for Father. It is finished and must be returned to the overseer tomorrow."

Meren lifted the sheet to reveal a copy of an old collection of wisdom handed down from scribe to scribe for centuries. He let the papyrus fall.

"You say nothing of your father's death. Earlier you were ready to blame Beltis for that and for the theft."

"Ah, Lord Meren, forgive me, but I never blamed Beltis for Father's killing." Djaper furrowed his brow. "But as I think upon the idea ... Beltis might ..."

"I don't like maidenly fluttering," Meren said. "Speak plainly."

Again Djaper's wide-open eyes lowered, and he

blushed. "Beltis is a woman of great appetite. She has come to my bed seeking pleasure of me, and—forgive me, lord—but it is distasteful to speak of such a thing. But Lord Meren has perhaps discovered the concubine's nature himself."

Meren only stared at Djaper.

"It may be," Djaper said when he realized he wouldn't get an answer, "it may be that Beltis decided that she wanted Father's goods and a younger man at the same time. Oh, not that I am fool enough to think she'd want me without the goods."

Djaper laughed, and Meren couldn't help smiling. The young man was laughing at himself, and such humility was admirable. Meren turned away from Djaper.

"You may arrange proper care for your father's body soon." With a nod he left Djaper. He closed the door behind him, then opened it again. Sticking his head inside the room, he caught Djaper as he was collapsing, loose-limbed, on the couch. "You know I will examine the copy of your father's will that rests in the House of Life."

Djaper rolled gracefully to the floor on his knees and bent his neck. "Yes, lord, I know."

"I'm not surprised."

Meren slammed the door shut and stood looking at it while he rubbed his chin. He would have to send men to check on the activities of the two brothers, but he didn't think Djaper had lied. Not about things that could be proven false. No, Djaper was much too clever to lie unless he lied well. But Meren wasn't convinced that the young man was as tranquil as he seemed. How could he be, having a father like Hormin? His *ka* should be shriveled with the heat of anger at being humiliated constantly by a man less intelligent than himself.

The scent of heavily spiced perfume intruded upon

Meren's thoughts. He sniffed and looked at Iry-nufer. The man was watching him, waiting for an opportunity to speak.

"The concubine was here," Meren said.

"Yes, my lord. She hovered about, but left when she saw me."

"Anyone else?"

"No, lord."

"Then come."

Meren set off for the chamber of Imsety. One last examination and he could go home. Kysen might be waiting for him with his news of the questioning of those of the Place of Anubis. It could be that Hormin's murder had nothing to do with his family and instead was related to one of the priests or embalming workers. It was just this possibility that had sent the old Controller of Mysteries into a fit and made him appeal to Meren in the first place.

Imsety was also guarded. As he left Iry-nufer and the other man at the door, Meren heard the scrape of metal against stone. Iry-nufer heard it too. The guard slipped past Meren, putting his body between his master and Imsety. He drew his scimitar and shouted at Imsety. Meren stepped to the side and saw Hormin's oldest son squatting on the floor, a whetstone and knife in his hands. He was gaping at Iry-nufer.

Iry-nufer hefted the scimitar. "I said drop the knife."

The blade clattered to the floor, but Iry-nufer wasn't satisfied.

"Your forehead to the floor. Spread out your arms."

When his victim was prone, Iry-nufer picked up the knife. He looked at Meren, who jerked his head toward the door. Iry-nufer left, uttering a threat in Imsety's direction.

"You may rise," Meren said.

Imsety raised himself to a sitting position and stuttered an apology.

"Where did you get the knife?"

"There are many in that pot, lord." Imsety pointed to a pottery jar by his bed. "Household knives, I hone them. The work—my hands." Imsety stopped; Meren waited, but the man had evidently said as much as he could or would.

"You like to work with your hands?" Meren asked.

"Yes, lord. Father, this house, the fighting." Imsety's big shoulders heaved with a sigh.

Meren waited, again in vain. "The work takes your thoughts from sorrow and anger."

"Yes, lord."

"Tell me, Imsety. Does everyone have to supply the words you don't say, or is it that you fear me?"

"I have many thoughts, lord, but my tongue, it is clumsy."

It was like plowing a stony field, but Meren dragged the story of the last day from Imsety. It was much the same as Djaper's, except that Imsety's day was spent in the company of his mother. The man seemed more concerned with the imminent harvest than with the death of his father, and he kept asking when he could go home.

"When I have the murderer," Meren said for the third time.

"It's Beltis. She killed Father."

"And dragged him to the riverbank, tossed him in a skiff, and hauled him to the Place of Anubis?"

Imsety nodded eagerly. "Caught her stealing."

"You wish me to believe that if Hormin caught Beltis stealing his treasure that there wouldn't be a fight as noisy as Thebes on a feast day?"

"One of the scribes."

Meren's head was beginning to pain him. "What are you talking about?"

"Bakwerner."

"Do you know anything about your father's murder, Imsety?"

"Bakwerner hates Father."

"I will concern myself with Bakwerner, not you." By this time Meren found himself grinding his teeth. "I want to know if Hormin was as cruel to you as he was to Djaper. He must have been, or he wouldn't have refused you the farm you work so hard to preserve."

Imsety shrugged and stared at Meren.

"You'd better say something."

"I never listened to Father."

Meren waited fruitlessly. After a few minutes during which Imsety stared at him and he tried not to toy with his dagger, Meren spoke.

"Never listened to him? What do you mean, curse you?"

"Since I was a naked child, I never listened to Father's hot words."

"Don't stop talking," Meren said.

"Ugly words, Father, they aren't important. The land is important. And Djaper. Not Father."

"And your mother."

"Mother loves Djaper."

Never had he been more grateful for having three chattering daughters. Meren closed his eyes and prayed to several gods for patience. Talking to Imsety was taking twice as long as it had with anyone else. There had been times, before he adopted Kysen, when he'd asked the gods why the girls couldn't have been boys. Now he would make a sacrifice to the goddess of childbirth.

Meren opened his eyes and caught Imsety staring at him. The young man's face was as expressionless as a figure painted on a temple wall. But a transitory flicker in Imsety's eyes set off the baying of hunting dogs in Meren's heart. Crocodiles often basked in the sun, still and placid, with no evidence of life in their bodies except for that brief, telltale lift of an eyelid that revealed a mindless hunger for flesh.

"You said neither you nor Djaper saw your father leave the house during the night."

Imsety gazed at Meren and made no attempt to avoid meeting Meren's stare. "No, lord. I never saw him."

That direct manner, it was a match for Djaper's ingenuousness. And it posed a difficulty. For in Meren's experience, the best liars, those whose hearts were filled with deceit, made a practice of meeting the eyes of those they deceived in just such a direct manner, while the innocent often foundered on their own lack of experience with evil. They quavered, faltered, and cast down their eyes. He would have to be Anubis, weigher of hearts at the soul's judgment, to decipher honesty based solely upon the face and habits of a man.

"Aren't you afraid that your father's murderer may harm you, Imsety?"

"No, Lord Meren. Why would he?"

"That is a question I've asked myself," Meren said. "And I'll find an answer. And if you should begin to fear, remember the ancient writings that tell us that justice lasts for an eternity and walks into the graveyard with its doer."

6

Kysen escaped the house without further damage to his ears. He made his way to a long, low building at the rear of the compound, which lay between the house and the barracks and stables. In it his father had established the headquarters for his duties as one of the Eyes and Ears of Pharaoh. There were workrooms for Nebamun, the physician-priest, and the scribes who kept records of the cases that came under Meren's hand, and two rooms for the count and his son.

Nebamun had finished his examination of the body by the time Kysen reached him. He was in the library consulting astrological charts and rubbing his shaved head in thought as he read. Kysen leaned on the doorsill.

"He died of the knife wound, didn't he?"

Nebamun looked up from the papyrus he'd spread across his crossed legs. "Assuredly. There was no sign of poison, and anyway, there was all that blood. But look at the writings for the day Hormin was born. They foretell a happy life."

"Do they say anything about his death?"

"No." Nebamun rolled up the papyrus and shook his head. "The men say there were no marks of the use of magic in the drying shed, and I found none on the body. He bit his fingernails, so I doubt if anyone could collect them for use in a spell. But there's always hair. We'll have to see what Lord Meren finds at his house."

"I can't think of any magic more potent than being stabbed with an embalming knife," Kysen said. "You'll send the body back to the embalmers for purification and treatment?"

"Yes, but you know his *ka* is likely to be wandering lost since he was dispatched by violence in so sacred a place. It will take powerful spells to restore his soul to his body."

Kysen didn't answer. He'd had to become accustomed to dealing with disturbed spirits just as he'd accepted that he would always meet evil. It was the price of being the son of the king's intelligencer. Yet sometimes dealing with malevolence made him feel contaminated. There'd been the time when that Babylonian merchant went mad and killed all those tavern women after raping them. He'd almost wished his father would relinquish his post by the time the merchant was caught.

After dictating his own observations to one of the scribes in the library, Kysen went to his father's office in search of the boxes containing Hormin's possessions and objects from the place of his death. He was lifting one of them from the floor to a worktable when he heard Meren's voice at the door.

"By the demons of the underworld, that is a family of cobras."

Kysen looked up and grinned. Even angry, Meren hardly looked old enough to be his father. At thirty-four he still kept the figure of a charioteer, and silver refused to appear in his cap of smooth black hair. Kysen's friends teased him that he would never get another wife because all the court maidens vied with each other for Meren's attention.

"Disturbed your plumb line, did Hormin's family?" Kysen asked.

Meren frowned at Kysen and stalked into the room. He dropped into his favorite ebony chair, slouched down in it, and cursed again. Kysen watched Meren drum his fingers on the arm of the chair, saw his features relax and then grow worried.

"You're staring at me," Kysen said.

"Mmmm."

Kysen pressed his lips together and pretended to straighten the lid of the box in front of him. He stilled when Meren spoke.

"You know about the village of the tomb makers."

"The water carrier told me."

"Did he recognize you?" Meren asked.

"He's new to the village," Kysen said. He let his gaze roam about the room, touching stacks of papyri, a water jar. "His father serves the painter Useramun. I remember Useramun. His hips wiggled when he walked, and he was always throwing tantrums if the plaster on tomb walls wasn't smooth enough for his paint."

"Any evil that touches the servants of the Great Place is important to Pharaoh. They're probably not involved, but I must make sure."

Rounding the worktable, Kysen took a stool near his father. "We can send for the chief scribe in the morning."

"You know that's not what I want to do."

"You want to go to the village?" Kysen flushed when his father lifted one of his straight brows. Meren could make him feel foolish more easily with a lift of those eloquent brows than by using a thousand words.

"I don't want to go," Kysen said.

"I can't do this, Ky. Word would be all over Thebes in minutes if I went there. Half the court would dog my steps out of curiosity or to make sure I didn't interfere with the work on their tombs. And how much do you think I'll get out of the scribes and artisans?"

"Little," said Kysen. "Oh, you don't have to tell me. I know. I'm the one who speaks their language. I'm the one who knows them—at least, I did know them. It's been ten years."

"Perhaps it will do you good to go back."

Kysen shot to his feet so quickly that his stool toppled. Ignoring it, he glared at his father, turned away, and placed both hands flat on the worktable.

"The fire pits of the netherworld, that's what that place was to me," Kysen said. "It's taken all this time for me to restore my *ka*, and you want me to go back there. You know what it was like. You saw me when Father tried to sell me in the streets of Thebes—the welts, the bruises so black I'd have been invisible on a moonlit night."

Rising, Meren went to Kysen. Kysen started when his father put a hand on his.

"You haven't seen your blood father since that day. Ky, I think facing him has become a great fear in your heart, and it grows larger the longer you ignore it. Hate makes festering sores in your *ka*."

"Gods!" Kysen shook off Meren's hand. "Shouldn't I hate him? You said it wasn't my fault that he beat me, though he never touched my brothers. It took you three years to convince me of my innocence, but I tell you, if I go back there, he'll make me see the ugliness within my heart."

"There is no ugliness in your heart. It's in Pawero's heart. Face him, Ky. You're no longer an eight-year-old child and helpless. Ah, you didn't think I knew your greatest fear. Go back to the village. You need to face Pawero, if only to make him admit his guilt."

"And while I'm chastising my monster of a father, I'm to spy on the villagers."

"Like a dutiful son," Meren said.

"This dutiful son remembers setting fire to the bed of your oldest daughter."

"And does he also remember copying chapters from *The Book of the Dead* for three months afterward?"

Kysen had been leaning against the worktable. He snorted and bent to right the fallen stool. When he was finished, he found his father standing beside him, studying him with that compassionate yet determined expression that had become so familiar. Meren had decided what was best for him, and nothing Kysen could say would change his heart.

"When do I go?"

"Tomorrow morning," Meren said. "I'll send word to the lector priest not to let the water carrier go home for a while. It may take a few days to question everyone without revealing what you're about."

"What if they know who I am—to you?"

Meren said, "They don't."

"What do you mean?"

Resuming his seat in the ebony chair, Meren grimaced. "I hadn't meant to tell you, but I've kept watch over the doings of your father and brothers. And I told him not to reveal who bought you. No one knows who you are now."

Kysen walked away from Meren to stand with his back against a wall. Hugging himself, he studied the man to whom he owed so much.

"I could kill him."

"You won't," Meren said calmly.

Making fists with both hands, Kysen forced himself to go on. "Sometimes, when Remi tries my patience to the breaking point, sometimes I almost—sometimes I want to—something happens to me. A demon takes possession of my *ka*, and I almost raise my hand to him." Kysen waited for condemnation with his head bowed.

"But you don't. You've never hit Remi, and you won't. Not until he is old enough to understand such punishment, and then you'll be fair and kind, for that is your nature."

Kysen raised his head and met his father's smiling gaze. "I want to hurt Pawero as he hurt me."

"Perhaps when you go to the tomb-makers' village you'll see that the good god has cast judgment on your behalf already." Meren stood up and led Kysen to the door. "It's time you abandoned this undeserved guilt and—"

Shock wiped all expression from Meren's face. Eyes focused on something Kysen couldn't see, his mouth opened, and air hissed between his lips as he drew in a breath.

"Listen to me," Meren said. "Ordering you to abandon guilt when I . . ."

"Father?"

"Leave me, Ky."

"But—"

"Now."

Kysen slipped away, leaving Meren standing in the doorway transfixed by thoughts he wouldn't share.

In the wharf market of Thebes, lines of booths covered with cloths flashed bright colors in the afternoon sun like the scales of fish glistening in a reflection pool. One stall boasted fresh waterfowl trussed up and dangling from square frames. The naked bodies of two pintails parted to reveal the sweaty nose of a man. The owner of the nose remained behind the strings of birds with only it and his eyes showing, and he darted glances about the crowded street.

The charioteer had been following him since he'd left the office of records and tithes. Bakwerner's mouth was dry, and he licked his cracked lips. Wiping a drop of sweat from his nose, he realized that evil had stalked him since he'd left those records on Hormin's shelf. Nothing he'd done since had warded off the unlucky events of the past day and night.

He had to escape the notice of the charioteer. Count Meren knew more than he had revealed. Why else would he set a watcher upon an innocent scribe? There! That was the man who followed him. Bakwerner shrank back behind the duck bodies. The owner of the stall cast a wary glance at him, so he pretended to examine a basket of pigeons. When he looked again, the charioteer's back was turned. Bakwerner dropped the basket, sidled past a booth filled with nuts and melons, and broke into a run.

Dodging a cart filled with dried dung and skirting a flower seller, he gained the shadows of an alley and worked his way into the city. Every tall man, every figure wearing bronze made him jump or dart into a doorway. With each false scare, his fear increased. The more he feared, the more he sweated. Rivulets of perspiration tickled their way from beneath his wig, down his face, and over his shoulders. His kilt was damp.

Since he took no time to wipe away the sweat, he first saw the house of Hormin through a blur of salty perspiration. The sight of the house burst the last of his restraint and he darted across the street and into the reception hall. Babbling at servants, he soon found himself in the presence of the wife.

"What are you doing here? What do you want?"

"Shhhh, mistress, we might be watched."

Hormin's wife scowled at him. "You mean someone's watching you?"

"The lord's man."

"They think you're guilty." The woman opened her brown lips and screeched.

Bakwerner ducked his head, covering his ears. "Please! Don't. I want to see your sons. Where are they?"

The wife of Hormin paid no attention to him. She kept screeching, this time calling for Imsety. Bakwerner waved his hands in front of her face in a desperate attempt to shut the woman up.

"Don't touch me, you worm." Selket rushed to a water jar that rested in a corner, lifted it, and hurled it at Bakwerner.

Bakwerner hopped aside as the jar flew at him. It crashed against the wall behind him and water sprayed both him and Selket. Hormin's wife let out a noise that combined a growl and a scream. Serving maids poked their heads around a door.

Footsteps pounded behind Bakwerner. He was caught by the shoulder and slung around. A giant loomed over him. Imsety.

"He's guilty and he's come to murder us all," Hormin's wife cried.

"I only want to talk," Bakwerner said. "You'll be sorry if you don't listen to me."

Imsety shoved Bakwerner. "Get out."

"I know things, and you'll be sorry. Fetch that brother of yours. He thinks he's so brilliant, favored of Toth. Well, he's not going to take the favor of the master from me. Bring him in here, because I know things."

Like his mother, Imsety didn't listen. He pulled back a fist that would have made two of Bakwerner's and jabbed it into the scribe's belly. Bakwerner grunted, doubling over. Imsety kicked his exposed buttocks, and Bakwerner stumbled. The giant lifted his fist again, but Bakwerner scrambled out of the way. With a staggering trot he managed to gain the street before Imsety decided to chase him.

Concerned only with keeping his body intact, Bakwerner dashed through the streets and alleys of Thebes. Reaching the wharf again, he took the ferry back across the river. As the boat skimmed over the water, Bakwerner straightened his wig and searched the faces of the other passengers. Here and there he thought he caught someone looking at him, but all were strangers and could have no interest in him. Still, as he hopped to land on the west bank, he shivered. Possibly it was because the breeze had skimmed over his damp skin. Bakwerner turned about suddenly to try to catch someone looking at him. The crowd of passengers surged around him, paying him no heed.

Hands twitching, gooseflesh forming on his arms, Bakwerner made his way back to the office of records and tithes. All the senior scribes were gone for the day. He hadn't realized how late it was, but the sun, the boat of Ra, was hurling rays at the gold and electrum on the temples and obelisks across the river. Shadows were long, distorted fiends dancing on the baked walls of the office.

Bakwerner pretended to be busy while apprentices and young student scribes set the rooms in order, packing away records, ink pigments, reed pens. With the sound of the first cricket they were gone, and Bakwerner was left in peace to think of what to do next. He stood on the loggia worrying his lower lip with his teeth. He had to talk to that little scorpion Djaper. He wasn't going to lose place because of a youth with the charm of a dancing girl. The only reason he was being considered for the post of chief was because no one wanted Hormin in it. But everyone liked Djaper, and the young man was far too brilliant. Before, Hormin would have had to be elevated for Djaper to rise. Now Hormin was gone, and Djaper had to be stopped. But how was he going to do it?

As Bakwerner pondered, lines of men and youths employed in the offices of the vizier streamed past the loggia. Students with their bundles of scribal equipment raced by, threading their way between the slower adults. Here and there a bare-bodied urchin lurked in search of a susceptible target for begging. One of them darted up in front of the loggia and planted himself before Bakwerner.

"Be off with you," Bakwerner said.

"Got a message." A toe dug in the dirt of the street. The boy lifted his eyes to the sky as if searching for the right words. "Someone you want to see is out back. Behind the pile of ostraca."

"Who? Wait!"

The boy disappeared in the flocks of workers. Bakwerner stared after him, then searched the ebbing and flowing numbers before him. No one was paying any attention to him.

Djaper. It had to be Djaper. The young fool had finally realized they had to talk. Bakwerner walked around the office to the back courtyard where deliveries of records were made. At the rear of the court was the pile of discarded limestone flakes, temporary records used to compile the permanent tax rolls and lists of exempt temple lands and citizens. It had grown taller than the height of two men since the beginning of the year.

Bakwerner approached the pile, but hesitated when he found no one visible.

"Who's there?"

There was no answer. The wind picked up, blowing his kilt against his legs, and he heard the cries of urchins as they played in the street. In the distance he could hear the bawling of sheep.

"Djaper, you young viper, I'm not afraid of you."

Bakwerner waited and listened. The tip of a shadow appeared around the edge of the mountain of ostraca. It melted along the jutting shards and vanished. He heard the click of stone against stone as one of the flakes dislodged and tumbled from its place midway in the pile.

Bakwerner hurried around the end of the pile in pursuit of the shadow. His pace picked up when he encountered nothing but the fallen ostracon. Then the shadow appeared, snaking forward from behind him.

"Ha! Playing your stupid games—"

Something heavy banged into his skull. Stinging agony brought him to his knees, but he caught himself, palms pressed into dirt. He looked up to see the pointed edge of an ostracon poised over him. Bakwerner almost had time to scream before the stone smashed into his face.

Dictating his experiences at the house of Hormin banished Meren's thoughts of the past. After sending Kysen away, he had a scribe take down all his conversations with those involved with Hormin. His memory was accurate, and he'd found that having a scribe record happenings in the presence of those under suspicion often panicked them.

He was reading through the notes taken by Kysen and his men when a foul odor assaulted his nose. It came from beneath the worktable. Meren opened the box that lay under the table to reveal Hormin's soiled kilt. Picking it up by an edge, Meren draped the cloth on the table. Waste, dirt, and natron combined to give off the smell that had finally escaped the confines of the box. Meren took a knife, cut out a square of the kilt that contained the perfume stain, and put the kilt back in the box. Setting the container outside the room, he returned to study the scrap of linen.

The yellow smudges gave off that peculiar spicy odor he couldn't identify. There were many perfumes available in the Two Lands, so it wasn't surprising that this one was unfamiliar. But the scent was curious, probably expensive. He'd have to send the scrap of linen to a perfumer, but he was sure none of the bottles in Hormin's treasure room contained a scent like this.

In another box he found the obsidian embalming knife. The gilt wood haft was decorated with the figure of the jackal god Anubis, patron of embalmers, and the words "Dweller in the chamber of embalming, Anubis. He sets thee in order. He fastens thy swathings."

Meren set the knife on the worktable and said a brief spell of protection for himself. Whoever had used this sacred instrument either had no fear of the gods or had been so enraged that using the knife hadn't mattered. It was more likely that the latter had been the case. Still, those who stole from the dead must overcome their fear, and there had been many cases of tombs being robbed in the past. Criminals didn't seem to be able to anticipate the judgment of the gods or the horrible fate of one's *ka* being eaten by the monsters of the netherworld, as happened to the sinful after death.

Asses' dung! This murder was wrought with more evil than most. It occurred in a sacred place, the weapon was sacred, the victim was a servant of Pharaoh and had gone about inviting his own killing with his jackallike behavior. His family hated him, or had cause to want him dead. His fellow scribe Bakwerner hated him. Hormin had cast his net of malevolence so wide,

Meren wasn't sure it didn't include a few tomb makers or even that pitiful water carrier Kysen mentioned. If Hormin would undermine the work of a royal scribe like Bakwerner, what would he do to a mere artisan or a water carrier?

Meren was digging in a box for Hormin's signet ring, bracelet, and the heart amulet when the creak of a door hinge caused him to spin around. His hands full of papyrus rolls and ostraca, Kysen gave him a look of inquiry. Meren nodded his permission to enter.

"Today's reports," Kysen said. "And wine."

Mutemwia followed him in with a tray and left them settled in chairs with a flagon between them.

"I was just looking at Hormin's possessions." Meren held out the signet ring. It had a flat bezel with a tiny inscription of Hormin's name. The bracelet bore the man's title as well as his name, and the workmanship was good.

Kysen gestured to include all of Hormin's things. "None of it is unusual for a scribe of Hormin's standing. His clothing was of good, though not the best, quality, as well."

"I know. But you didn't see his treasure room. The man hoarded, Ky, so we mustn't overlook any sign his possessions may give us." Meren wrapped his hands around his wine goblet and sighed. "I don't know. There's something wrong, but I can't decide what it is. I need to juggle."

"Oh no," Kysen said. "Not while I'm here." He bent down and gathered up a handful of records, shoving them at his father. "These will distract you."

There was silence while they both read.

Kysen said, "The city police report the arrest of a tavern keeper for the prostitution of children."

Meren's mouth tightened, but he kept his gaze on the

reports in his hand. "The judges will dismember him."
He tapped the papers with one finger. "A tax collector
has beaten a peasant to death. He was punishing the
man for repositioning the boundary stones on his land,
and he hit the man's head instead of his back. And one
of the mortuary priests of the temple of Amunhotep the
Magnificent is accused of diverting grain from the treasury for his own use."

"Stupid," Kysen said.

"What?"

"The mortuary priest is stupid. One doesn't steal
from the father of the reigning Pharaoh; one steals from
the mortuary temple of an older king or prince who's
been forgotten."

"True. Anyway, the only other report from the necropolis is that another laborer has fallen to his death.
He was on his way from the nobles' cemetery to the
Valley of the Kings. I think that's the third accident this
year."

Kysen waved a papyrus roll. "The vizier has sent
word that the vassal prince Urpalla wants more of Pharaoh's gold to buy mercenaries to fight the Hittites."
Kysen stopped when his father groaned and threw a papyrus bearing the royal seal to the floor.

"What's wrong?"

"May the fiends of the netherworld take her," Meren
said. "One of Pharaoh's half sisters, Princess Nephthys,
she's pregnant and won't name the father."

Meren almost shuddered at the possibilities opened up
by this latest disaster. The right to the throne of Egypt
passed through the female line. Nephthys was the daughter of a minor royal wife and Amunhotep the Magnificent, but women with less royal blood than she had tried
to claim the throne for their sons.

"Shall I burn that?" Kysen asked, indicating the report on the princess. Even at home they couldn't afford to leave writings from the king lying about. He took the paper from Meren and touched it to the flame of an alabaster lamp.

As he dropped the last curling bit of papyrus, Irynufer walked into the room and saluted. Eyes bleary from lack of sleep, he wasted no breath with polite salutations.

"Lord, one of Hormin's servants saw Bakwerner at dusk on the night of the murder. He was skulking in the alley next to the house when she passed by on her way home, but when he saw her, he left."

"She's sure he left?" Meren asked.

"Yes, but then she went home, so he could have come back. But that isn't all. Bakwerner visited the family of Hormin after we left them. He eluded the man set to watch him and came creeping about, dodging into doorways and out until he was sure there were no strangers about. Looking for one of us, I'm sure." Iry-nufer gave Kysen a self-satisfied smile. "When I saw him, I found one of the maids and told her to listen to what he was saying."

Meren said, "It couldn't have been too difficult a task given the way those people yell."

"The lord is wise," Iry-nufer said. "He started out talking to the wife of Hormin. The maid couldn't hear everything, but she thought he was pleading. Then the old woman screamed, and that older brother came in and yelled at Bakwerner, shouting that he was here to cast blame for the murder upon the family. I heard the noise and ran into the house. Bakwerner was yelling, but Imsety beat him, and Bakwerner scuttled out of the house like a beetle chased by a goose."

Meren leaned back in his chair and stared at the ceiling. "Where was the young one?"

"The young one?"

"Djaper." Meren sat up and eyed Iry-nufer. "Where was Djaper?"

"He never appeared. Used to such commotion, I suppose. I left when I saw that no one was going to be killed."

Meren said, "I want to know where Djaper was when his brother was fighting with Bakwerner. And I'll speak to you later about this incident, Iry-nufer."

"Anything else?" said Kysen.

"No, lord. The man assigned to Bakwerner arrived and followed him back to the office of records and tithes. It was getting late, so when my replacement arrived, I came to report."

Iry-nufer bowed and left. Meren watched Kysen crush ashes from the burned papyrus beneath his sandal. Neither said anything. Long silences often accompanied the reception of such news. He would be busy tomorrow, what with the problems at court and the murder inquiry. As for Kysen, when the sun came up he would go to the tomb-makers' village because he wanted to please Meren.

The door burst open and Meren's hand jumped to his dagger. Iry-nufer charged into the office followed by a youth, one of the apprentice charioteers. The youth was panting and leaned against the door.

"Lord," Iry-nufer said. "It's Bakwerner."

Meren and Kysen looked at each other. Meren's voice snapped with impatience.

"He's dead, isn't he?"

"Someone smashed his face in with an ostracon."

"The criminal?" Meren asked.

The youth had caught his breath and answered. "Gone, escaped over a wall hidden by the pile of ostraca behind the office of records and tithes. Reia was watching him from the corner of the building, but he disappeared behind the ostraca and never came out. By the time Reia decided something was wrong, it was too late."

"Very well," Meren said. "We'll come at once."

Kysen fell into step with him, and Meren glanced his way.

"I had a feeling the evil would spread," Kysen said. "Whoever killed in the Place of Anubis is terrified."

"Or possessed of more audacity than a thousand Libyan bandits. Bakwerner saw something, of course. I could have dragged him here and threatened him, but I was waiting for him to panic."

"You were right. He did panic." Kysen took note of his father's frown. "Even the high priest of Amun couldn't have foretold what would happen."

"I can only pray that we catch the evil one before he strikes again," Meren said. He shook his head as they reached the front door. "You know how it is when a beast tastes human blood, what happens to a man when he learns how easy it is to murder."

"The ancients say one becomes a butcher whose joy is slaughter," said Kysen.

"And the butcher is loose among us."

7

The God Ra burst into life in the east, bringing light and life, as Kysen boarded the supply skiff headed for the tomb-makers' village. The boat's owner followed, and they glided out into the channel headed west. The canal was one of many cut into the earth to bring water to fields on either side of the Nile. In the distance peasants bent over another canal bank and emptied baskets of soil into its collapsed side. If the canals weren't kept in good repair, life-giving water receded. Without such irrigation the lush green fields would vanish, replaced by the creamy desolation of the desert.

Kysen glanced down at the plain kilt wrapped around his hips. Last night he had decided that he would return to the tomb-makers' village as one of his father's minions rather than as his son. Meren had said that it was unlikely that he'd be recognized, even by his father—after all, he'd been a child when he last saw the village. Thus he'd left behind his belts of turquoise and gold, his fine leather sandals, his broad collars of malachite and electrum.

He shifted uneasily on the plank that was his seat. His leg brushed a bag of grain, grain meant for the tomb-makers' village. Most of the village supplies were shipped in from temple and royal storehouses; unlike most villagers, the artisans lived not at the edge or in the midst of cultivation, but in a bare, rocky desert valley south of the Valley of the Queens. Kysen remembered his father's grudges against the foremen and scribes, for they received a great ration of Pharaoh's grain.

His father. Would Pawero recognize him? Would his brothers? If not, Kysen decided not to reveal himself. One of his first lessons under Meren had been in how not to reveal what he knew. The gazelle does not seek the lion in the midst of the herd. It looks outward, and ignores the animal at its side. Thus it would be with the artisans. They would guard secrets from Meren's agent, but fail to conceal from him things he couldn't be expected to know.

There was another advantage. From the protection of his facade as a royal servant, he would be safe from Pawero. Kysen rubbed his upper arms and stared into the ripples of water caused by the skiff. What had possessed him to think such a thought?

Pawero was almost ten years older than Meren—an old man by now. An old man no longer strong enough to backhand his son, especially a son grown tall and trained as a warrior. Slick, oily rage curled a black trail through Kysen's body and snaked around his heart. He shook his head and drew in a sharp breath. With the scimitar of his will, he cut through the tendrils of wrath.

Rage had no place in the work he was to do. His attention jolted back to his surroundings as the skiff bumped against a small dock. Clambering ashore, Kysen pulled the strap of the bag that held his possessions over his shoulder. A line of donkeys and their handlers huddled nearby, waiting for the grain. He could have gone ahead along the trail that climbed bald hills and descended into the valley that held the village, but he wasn't supposed to know the way.

Soon he was walking beside a donkey, leaning forward as the trail slanted up and darted into the heart of the lifeless rock that soon would glow with the day's killing heat. Somehow the journey was too short. In much less than an hour he topped the summit of a hill and gazed out into the rubble-strewn valley. He forgot to breathe. A high whitewashed wall surrounded the village, and he could see the flat roofs of the houses that flanked either side of the one main street. Kysen almost stumbled as a donkey jostled him. He'd forgotten how enclosed the village was. There was only one entrance in the wall, only one way in or out.

In spite of the rapidly growing heat, his skin grew cold. Vague memories crowded upon him—the death of his mother when he was small, his brothers, an older boy called Useramun, already a brilliant painter, the old scribe of the village who was now dead. But he couldn't remember their faces.

Once Meren had taken him home, he'd made a deliberate decision to wipe from his thoughts all trace of his old life. He'd stuffed old memories, good and bad, into a sarcophagus of black diorite and dropped the lid. Now it was difficult to lift that heavy lid and release the memories. He seemed to recall things better than people. The village looked so much smaller than he remembered.

One of the supply men elbowed his companion and pointed to another trail, a white scar in the rocks of the hills farther west and north.

"He fell where the path takes a sharp turn and skirts the Cliff of the Hyenas. Broke his neck. You can still see the blood on the rocks at the foot of the cliff."

Suddenly alert, Kysen spoke up. "Someone fell from a cliff?"

"Yes, master." It was the owner of the donkeys who

answered. "A quarryman. Last week. It happens some-times, may the revered Osiris protect us. A man grows careless after years of climbing these hills. He missteps, puts his foot on a loose rock too near the edge." The man slapped his palms together. "Smashes onto a valley floor and breaks like a melon."

"Ah yes. I heard in the dock market that a quarryman was killed. Was anyone with him?"

"No, master, else they would have told the fool not to go so near the edge."

Kysen heard the disguised contempt in the man's voice. It was obvious he was considered one of the soft, pampered city officials who knew little of real work. No doubt the whole village would take the same attitude. Many of those who worked in the vast royal and temple bureaucracies were corrupt. Scandals often arose about functionaries who took bribes and cheated honest folk. A few had ended up on Meren's list of murder victims in the office at home.

Refraining from comment, Kysen accompanied the grain supplies down to the village. He dropped back be-hind the last man as they approached the village tem-ples, small replicas of the great stone structures on the east bank. He glanced at the hillsides to his right and left. Pierced with tomb shafts, they contained the resting places of the artisans' ancestors, his ancestors. To the southwest he could just make out the white-painted chapel that stood before the tomb of his family.

Laughter distracted him. A group of people emerged from the shadows of the main street. This road was so narrow one could touch the houses on either side of it. At the head of the crowd walked a man. He stepped past the gate in the wall, talking rapidly all the while. The two women who flanked him burst into renewed mirth while the man lapsed into a silent smile.

Kysen noted the scribe's kit dangling from his right hand, the roll of papyrus in his left. This was Thesh, scribe of the Great Place. Scribe—one of the most noble of all professions. Scribe—the profession that opened its arms to any boy, peasant or noble, who possessed a heart clever enough to memorize over seven hundred hieroglyphs, their corresponding cursive script, and their use.

Kysen himself could read and write. He wasn't fool enough to think the ability made him a scribe, for scribes managed accounts, commanded laborers, surveyed an entire kingdom, preserved the sacred texts of the gods. As a scribe, Thesh would handle matters of law and religion, economy and labor.

Thesh and his train of followers reached the long, open pavilion in front of the village entrance. The scribe called a greeting to the supply men before seating himself on a reed mat. The women gathered behind him while the grain was unloaded and set before Thesh. Kysen remained behind a donkey, watching. As scribe, Thesh equaled in importance the two foremen of the artisans, and was probably the most influential man in the village. He would have dealt with Hormin.

Having unstrung his scribe's kit from its knotted cord, Thesh was instructing a boy in the mixing of ink as the last of the grain was unloaded. Now that the supply men had stopped moving about, several of the women noticed him and gave him curious looks. Kysen held back. Thesh looked up from the papyrus he'd been studying, and his gaze fastened on Kysen at once.

He expected to be beckoned peremptorily to stand before the scribe. Instead, Thesh allowed the papyrus to snap closed. Setting it aside, he held Kysen's gaze, furrowed his brow, then rose and walked over to this newcomer. Kysen felt a stab of apprehension. Thesh couldn't know him. Thesh was new to the village. He'd taken up residence years after Kysen had been sold.

"May the gods protect thee," Thesh said.

Kysen nodded, surprised. Thesh had greeted him as one greets a superior. What had given him away?

The scribe's lips twitched, but he didn't smile. Kysen suspected the man knew he was discomfited.

"I am Seth, servant of the Eyes and Ears of Pharaoh, Friend of the King, the Count Meren."

It seemed the rock cliffs echoed with Kysen's father's name; silence dropped over the crowd beneath the pavilion, shroudlike and startling. He scanned the faces of Thesh and his companions but perceived no fear or guilt, only open surprise. His glance settled on Thesh.

The man had the look of a scribe. His skin wasn't so dark as those who labored continually in the sun. His hands were smooth and uncallused. Eyes bright black with intelligence, he resembled a sleek raven. His nose was straight as the side of a pyramid, as was his back. Kysen noted no slackness of belly or limb, and a certain artistry of face that told him Thesh was accustomed to having a train of women at his back.

Thesh inclined his head, respect to an equal, and Kysen breathed more easily. He had been taken for a servant, the servant of a great man, but a servant. He couldn't delay an explanation any longer.

"The scribe Hormin has been murdered. He was known to have visited this village yesterday, and I have come to inquire about his business and his movements."

Thesh's eyes widened at the news. The women behind him drew closer.

"Murdered?" the scribe asked.

Surprise, but no dismay. Kysen nodded. "In the Place of Anubis." Saving Kysen the trouble, Thesh flicked his hand at the women. They receded, along with the supply men, back into the shadows of the village where they could be heard whispering together in the main street. His brow furrowed, Thesh led Kysen to the reed mat. They settled upon it, facing each other.

"Who would do murder in the Place of Anubis?" Thesh asked quietly. "What unnatural carrion would offend the gods in such a manner?"

"You do not ask who would want to kill Hormin."

"One of his family?"

Kysen leaned back, placed his palms flat on the mat, and surveyed Thesh. "What makes you say this?"

"Naught of importance." Thesh's face resumed its humorous lines. "I bethought me that of all the persons who might wish to do him harm, those who were under his hand the most would be the most tempted."

He wouldn't smile, despite the temptation. The cleverness of the answer aroused Kysen's respect.

"Tell me of Hormin and his dealings with the artisans of the Great Place."

"Hormin had permission to build his tomb near the nobles' cemetery, and he'd commissioned work from us."

"And it was about these commissions that he came yesterday?"

Thesh failed to answer at once. He picked up a water pot and poured into the inkwells on his palette. Stirring with a stick to mix the ink, he went on.

"Yesterday was Hormin's day for chasing his concubine, as you no doubt know."

Kysen said nothing while the scribe placidly stirred black ink, then progressed to the red. Thesh lifted his head then, and quirked a smile.

"Beltis considers herself to be as great an artisan as the Kaha family or Useramun, the master painter. In the practice of her art, she sometimes visits her parents. In order to drive Hormin mad with fear that one of us will catch her eye, or worse, some nobleman. Hormin is—was—a jealous man."

Kysen was about to ask how Thesh knew of this jealousy when, over the scribe's shoulder, he saw a woman coming toward them from the houses. She was carrying a tray of food, but moving slowly, as if her legs were filled with sand. She reached the pavilion, knelt, and set the tray between Thesh and Kysen.

Her slow movements had deceived him. She wasn't an old woman, but then neither was she young. She had the wide face of the south, with full lips and a vanishing chin. An unremarkable face set atop a slim body and strong legs. If he had seen her from the back and then from the front, he would have been disillusioned, for the body promised and the face disappointed.

Thesh was pouring beer into cups without looking at the woman. "Seth, servant of Count Meren, this is my wife, Yemyemwah, called Yem."

Kysen nodded to Yem, who ducked her head at him.

"Yem, Hormin has been murdered, and Seth has come to divine his movements yesterday."

Yem's fleshy lips pressed together. "And the woman?"

The words had been said in a flat, dull voice, and yet Kysen felt the eagerness with which she awaited the answer. This woman longed for the death of Beltis the concubine. Kysen immediately glanced at Thesh, who had paused in the middle of the act of presenting a cup to Kysen. His hand remained suspended, and Kysen could see his fingers tighten around the rim until the flesh turned white.

"What woman?" Kysen asked.

"The whore."

"Yem!"

"Mean you the concubine?" Kysen asked, taking the cup from Thesh.

Again Yem nodded.

"Only Hormin has been murdered. Do you know anything pertaining to Hormin and his doings, mistress?"

Yem darted a look at her husband. Thesh was trying not to glare at her. He snatched a loaf of bread from the tray and ripped it in half. The violence with which he did so betrayed him, and he seemed to realize it. He dropped the bread and waved at Yem in dismissal. As she rose, Kysen lifted his hand.

"A moment, mistress, to answer my question."

"I know naught but that she came here to see her parents yesterday, and then he came for her and they fought. The whole village knew this. It is a game she plays. Beltis plays many—games. I saw him rushing down the main street carrying a small wicker box under his arm, a bribe, no doubt, to get her home. They had one of their donkey-braying arguments. She could make the pillars of a temple go deaf. The fighting stopped, and I never saw them again, for I had bread to bake and spinning to complete."

"My thanks, mistress."

Yem bowed and left them, slogging her way toward the houses as if she waded through a sea of mud. Kysen settled himself more comfortably, leaning part of his weight on his arm, picked up a chunk of bread, and lifted a brow at Thesh. The scribe took a sip of his beer, but when Kysen merely took a bite of his bread rather than launching into accusations, he sighed.

"I told you Beltis considered herself an artisan."

Kysen's gaze never faltered, and Thesh cleared his throat.

"Yem is a good woman, but we haven't been blessed

by the gods with children, and Yem is unhappy. We're both unhappy. Beltis is all laughter and fire and—"

"Did you have her yesterday?"

Thesh shook his head. "He came, just as Yem said. I could tell when she arrived that this was one of those times when she had other matters to attend to. He followed her here and they fought, as Yem said. After they reconciled, Hormin came to see me to have payments recorded to the account of the painter Useramun and to one of the sculptors. Then they went with Woser to see his tomb. I never saw them after that."

"And who were those among you who dealt with Hormin?"

"Beltis's parents of course, and the men who designed and built his tomb. Woser the draftsman and Useramun the master painter saw him the most."

"And did they deal well together?"

"Hormin never dealt well with anyone. He tormented poor Woser, who would rather be a dung carrier than a draftsman, and of course he hated Useramun."

Thesh stopped, flushed, and directed his gaze at the cliffs.

"Why?"

The scribe shook his head. "This is a question for the painter."

"It is a question for you, and I do not ask it to exercise my lips."

The snap in Kysen's voice caused Thesh to glance at him in surprise. Their gazes locked, and although Thesh was the older man, he looked away first.

"Useramun is not only a master painter. He is a man of pleasing appearance, one who does not mind risking his hide if his pleasure is furthered."

"Are you telling me that the concubine deliberately

came here to drive Hormin into a fit wondering if she was with you or Useramun?"

"I am still well, and so is Useramun. If he had more than suspicions, no doubt he would have ruined both of us. I have always believed Hormin thought Beltis was teasing him. He didn't have respect for her, for any woman, and never would have thought her clever enough to deceive him. Hormin was a fool."

"Perhaps," Kysen said.

He placed his cup on the tray and rose. Thesh did as well.

"I must remain here at least one night so that I may question all those you have mentioned."

"I am honored to offer my house for your comfort," Thesh said. "But surely we are not suspected of this villainy."

Kysen had his usual reply ready, but before he could speak, three people emerged from the village gate. His eye caught the movement, and he looked over Thesh's shoulder. A youth and two men. One old, two young. The old man moved slowly, his joints swollen, his progress aided by a walking stick. The sun gleamed off his bald head, and as he neared the pavilion Kysen could see the gray bristles of an unshaven beard.

The younger man next to him glanced at Thesh and Kysen curiously, and Kysen caught his breath. The face of his father stared back at him. Almond-shaped eyes with the shine of marble, plinthlike chin, unsmiling mouth. It was his brother Ramose. Who else could it be? Which meant that the other was Hesire and the unkempt old relic at his side was . . . Pawero.

Kysen jerked as Thesh touched his arm. "What? What say you?"

"Do you wish to speak with them? Talking to Pawero will be of little help. His health is bad, and he does little work now. Ramose and his brother Hesire are taking him to his farm south of the city. I can stop them."

"No." Kysen stopped, for he'd answered too quickly and too sharply. "No doubt they will return before I leave. Unless they had intimate dealings with Hormin, I will wait."

"No, they barely knew him, I think."

"Then, if you will conduct me to the man called Woser, I will see him next."

Thesh murmured his assent, and they left the shade of the pavilion. Before they reached the village gate, Kysen turned and glanced at his family. They hadn't recognized him. He was uncertain how he felt about that. The rest of his thoughts were confused, for the man who had loomed in his nightmares as a netherworld fiend was, in truth, a wrinkled, bent old wreck.

$\triangledown$

8

Meren jumped from his chariot, snapped an order to his driver to remain in the shade of a palm at the edge of the market, and began to thread his way toward the Street of the Ibex. His fury at Bakwerner's murder had cooled somewhat. He had no doubt that the scribe had been killed because of some secret knowledge. And he had little doubt that someone had been threatened by that knowledge, most likely someone in Hormin's family. But perhaps not; perhaps the visit to Hormin's family had been happenstance.

Meren's lips tightened as he remembered how little they'd learned from searching the area around the pile of ostraca. The packed earth yard had yielded no trace of the passage of Bakwerner or his murderer. The killer had left no signs at all when he vanished into the evening crowds.

Two murders. A killer who murdered swiftly, who dared the vengeance of the gods and the king. A killer who must be stopped before someone else died.

He saw the Street of the Ibex ahead, its intersection marked by an obelisk so old that the raised edges of its hieroglyphs were blurring. At a corner, in the shade of a broad stall, lounged one of his servants. The man saw him, glanced at the open door of a tavern, and came to meet him.

"Lord, the large brother is in the tavern. He came directly from the house."

"Did he see you? No, never mind getting offended. He didn't see you." Meren forced his sour temper away and gave the servant a smile and nod. "Well done. You may go home and rest."

"But, lord, I should accompany—"

"Gods, man! I need no nursemaid."

"Aye, lord, but—"

"Belabor me no longer," Meren said. "Have my charioteer follow. At a distance, mind you. That should satisfy your duty."

The man's furrowed brow smoothed and he retreated, bowing.

Meren had already forgotten the servant before he left. Perhaps Imsety was having a midday meal. If he didn't come out of the tavern soon, he would go in. He'd worn a simple headcloth and leather belt and no armbands to mark him as a noble or warrior. In the jostling crowds they wouldn't notice him.

He winced at the sound of a screeching monkey. A baboon leaped from the roof of a fruit seller's stall and scrambled after a boy clutching a melon. The fruit seller shouted and pointed at the boy, who laughed and tossed a basket over the monkey before vanishing. A few minutes passed, during which Meren saw his charioteer take up a position near a vendor of nuts. He nodded at the man, who gave him an almost imperceptible salute. It was one of the more irritating aspects of his station never to be allowed to venture out alone without causing his men and his servants both consternation and anxiety.

A cart rattled by, loaded with tall wine jars sealed with clay. Meren watched it pass the tavern as the hulking form of Imsety levered its way out the door. Meren turned his head to the side, moving back into the shadow of an awning.

As Imsety walked down the Street of the Ibex, Meren shoved away from the awning and merged with the shoppers and merchants. After a space, the charioteer followed Meren. Imsety moved leisurely, never glancing over his shoulder or to the side, and paused at a house fronted by a low mud-brick wall forming a small court. In the court under an awning sat a man at a table laden with jewelry. Behind the man lay a stoked furnace attended by two apprentices. With wooden tongs they lifted a vessel filled with molten metal and poured it into a mold.

Meren stopped near the wall and pretended interest in the woolen cloths of a Bedouin family. Imsety swung back the gate in the wall and approached the jeweler. Looming over the stall, he produced a glittering, beaded object. Meren held up a length of red cloth and peered over it as Imsety spread his possession before the jeweler: cylindrical beads in alternating rows of gold, red jasper, and lapis lazuli—Hormin's stolen prize. The merchant picked up the necklace and peered at the finials at each end, then muttered at Imsety.

Narrowing his eyes, Meren watched as the two appeared to haggle over a price. Finally the merchant scribbled a few words on a scrap of papyrus. Both he and Imsety put their names on it. Then Imsety placed the receipt in the waistband of his kilt and walked out of the courtyard. Meren turned his back as his quarry passed, retracing his steps down the Street of the Ibex.

Darting quickly into the jeweler's court, Meren grabbed the man's hand as it swept up the necklace from the table in front of him.

"What?" the man squawked. "Whatwhatwhat?"

"The necklace—what was your dealing with that young man about the necklace?"

"Only a small repair, good master. The finials need refinishing. Who are you? I like not your—"

The jeweler's mouth dropped open. His jaw hung slackly as Meren's charioteer appeared. His gaze darted from the whip and dagger at the warrior's belt to the leather and gold wristbands and neck guard.

"There is trouble, lord?"

Meren was already hurrying after the brother. He called over his shoulder, "Get the lapis and red jasper necklace and meet me at the chariot." As he left he heard the charioteer questioning the jeweler.

"Has the young man Imsety ever been to you before?"

"N-no, good master. He is a stranger."

Leaving the merchant still gaping at him, Meren hurried down the street in Imsety's wake. As he wove through the crowds he tried to spot Imsety's broad shoulders and head above the others in the street. He zigzagged around peddlers, children, and women laden with baskets; the delay at the jeweler's had given his quarry a head start. He plunged around a stack of pottery jars taller than himself, only to dodge behind them again upon seeing Imsety. He'd purchased a honey cake at a baker's stall and was devouring it whole.

Meren waited, then followed as Imsety turned a corner into one of the narrow side streets that intersected the main road. He approached the corner warily; beyond it the street, little more than an alley, zigged and zagged into darkness. Awnings stretched from rooftop to rooftop on many such pathways to protect travelers from the sun.

He edged around the corner, keeping close to the wall. The darkness caused his sight to blur for a moment before he could make out a stretch of emptiness. The buildings on either side crowded close, leaving room for no more than two people to walk abreast, and then only shoulder to shoulder. The lane turned sharply to the right about thirty paces from the corner. Imsety had already disappeared.

Meren slipped into the shadows and hurried to the next corner. Sliding around it, he found another short stretch ending in a turn to the left. He would have to increase his pace if he wasn't to lose Hormin's son in this maze. He paused briefly at the next corner, then plunged down the lane. By now the buildings were so close, the awnings so thick that it was hard to see. He neared the next turn, slowed.

Something grabbed him as he passed a doorway. A pair of sweaty hands fastened on his throat and squeezed. Meren felt blood rush to his head, surge, and nearly burst from his eyes. He was lifted off his feet as he clawed at the hands on his throat, twisting and writhing to no avail. Meren raised his arms, planting one fist against another. His strength ebbing, he rammed his elbow into the chest of the man behind him.

The hold on his throat loosened slightly. He had only moments before it tightened again for the last time. Going limp, Meren heard a grunt of satisfaction. His feet touched the ground as his attacker began to release him. He quickly made fists. Jabbing backward with his thumbs, he gouged at the man's eyes. He heard a yelp, and suddenly he was free.

Whirling around, Meren kicked a massive, bare stomach. The attacker grunted, buckled, and sank to his knees. He was about to punch the man when he slumped to the ground. Whipping around, Meren glanced about the darkened passage for further danger.

Perceiving no one else, Meren straightened from his

crouch. He brushed a hand through his hair and smoothed the folds of his kilt. The years as a charioteer and warrior still came to his aid. This wasn't the first time his training had saved him from danger encountered in his duties to Pharaoh.

He drew a dagger that hung from the belt at his waist. Leaning against a wall, he contemplated the groaning Imsety. The fool had risked death by attacking a nobleman and would be punished—but he would be questioned first. As he watched the man on the ground, his charioteer burst into the passage and slid to a halt. He glanced from Meren to his victim, snorted contemptuously, and went silent. Imsety rolled onto his back, then pushed himself to a sitting position and rubbed his eyes. He opened them. His teary gaze found Meren, and for once he found more than three words to say.

"My lord Meren! Merciful Amun, I am destroyed." Imsety struggled to his knees and held out a beseeching hand to Meren. "I thought you were a thief. I beg you, lord, please believe me."

Meren regarded Imsety without expression, allowing the young man to babble. Imsety was squinting at him, his eyes red. His massive shoulders hunched, and he groaned as Meren lounged silently against the wall.

"I am dead," Imsety said.

He crouched in the street before Meren. His head was bowed nearly to the ground in supplication. Meren heard him draw in a breath as he lifted his head to glance at the charioteer and saw the necklace bunched in the fist of the warrior. His features smoothed into blankness.

"Your clattering tongue has stilled," Meren said softly. "No matter. It will flap freely enough before you die."

Imsety closed his eyes briefly. Meren twitched his

dagger at Hormin's son, causing him to lurch to his feet.

"Come," Meren said. "It seems I'll sit in judgment of you before you go to the gods for theirs."

He had no trouble in shepherding the dispirited Imsety back to his chariot and to his headquarters. He had his guards throw Hormin's son into a holding room in the small barracks behind his office. Imsety remained there, nursing his fear, while Meren bathed and changed.

While his body servant arranged the folds of a fresh kilt around him, Meren wondered how Kysen was faring at the village of the tomb makers. He had encouraged his son to return to the place many times, only to relent in the face of the boy's pain. This murder had offered an occasion to insist that Kysen confront old Pawero and leave behind old and haunting memories.

Meren felt his body servant tug on his wrist. He held it out so that the boy could fasten a studded wristguard in place; his warrior's garb would further intimidate the hulking Imsety. When the last tie of his gilt leather corselet had been tightened across his chest, he slipped a dagger in his belt and held out his hand for a gold-handled chariot whip.

He had contemplated wearing a short sword, but discarded the idea. He wouldn't need it with his aides in attendance, and the sword would be too much. He preferred subtlety, though it would probably be lost on Imsety. Meren touched the gold band that held his head-cloth in place and dismissed the body servant. It was time to play the cruel aristocrat and strike fear into the heart of Imsety.

The barracks was a long, low building with a central hall. Meren entered the hall flanked by two aides to find several charioteers. Two guarded an interior door, while another sat by one of the support columns, mending a whip. Meren nodded at the sentries. They threw open the door, and one ducked inside the dark chamber. Imsety stumbled into the hall, shoved by the charioteer. Propelled by the guards, he lumbered over to Meren and fell to his knees when two hands shoved on his shoulders.

Meren slapped the coiled whip against his thigh deliberately. Imsety glanced at it. Meren caught his expression—one of dull resignation. He remained silent, his plan suddenly altered by this perception. Who had always obtained Imsety's cooperation? Not the brutal Hormin, but the clever Djaper. Meren gazed at the man on his knees while he held out the whip. An aide came forward to take it, while the other brought a chair.

He sat, never taking his gaze from Imsety. The man was obsessed with his farm. He wanted to go home. This Meren believed. What had Imsety been willing to do to obtain the farm and go home? Did he have the courage or the rashness to rob his own father? Meren drew his dagger. Laying it flat against his palm, he pretended to contemplate the iron blade. He'd taken it from a Hittite in a skirmish near Tyre. The handle bore a turquoise inlay and the pommel was of rock crystal. He watched the crystal reflect dim colors while he thought, then began to tap the flat of the blade against his palm.

"You're a fool, Imsety, and a stubborn one."

Imsety stirred, but he had regained his ability to keep silent.

"Yes, stubborn. But how stubborn will you remain if I give Djaper a taste of my whip instead of you?"

His jaw stiff, Imsety widened his eyes and stared at Meren, who smiled at him.

Meren looked at the aide beside his chair. "Abu, bring Djaper, son of Hormin, to me at once."

"No!" Imsety stretched out a hand to Meren, only to have it knocked aside by one of the guards. The other hit him on the side of the head, and he subsided back onto his heels. "Please, lord, I beg of you. Don't hurt Djaper."

Concealing his surprise, Meren watched Imsety struggle with some inner perplexity. The effort distorted the man's fleshy features. His thick lips skewed to the side, and great furrows appeared between his brows. Meren decided to push him again. He nodded to Abu, who turned to leave.

"I will tell you all!" Imsety said.

Meren glanced back at his victim as if in surprise. "Well?"

"We quarreled with my father." Imsety paused and wet his lips. "He would never have given me the farm. Not if he gained ten times the wealth he already had. We took the collar."

"When?"

"The night—the night he was killed."

"Come," Meren said. "Don't lose your newfound eloquence or I shall begin to think of sending for Djaper."

"That night, we had gone to the house of a friend to let our anger cool. We came home and went to our beds, but later—Djaper had thought of a plan. We would devise a false robbery."

"You looted Hormin's room," Meren said.

Imsety nodded.

"And were to sell some of the booty."

"I would have purchased my own farm." Imsety said this last with a shrug. "But the necklace was broken and needed repair."

At a look from Meren, Abu produced the necklace, the beads cascading into Meren's hand. Most collars had end pieces made in the shape of animal heads that fastened together, but each edge of this one instead bore only the thin, smooth gold pin by which the finial should have been attached. Also missing was the metal counterpoise that should have hung down the wearer's back to hold the heavy collar in place.

Meren handed the collar back to Abu, then snapped at Imsety. "You saw Hormin leave the house late after going to his concubine. That is why you did your stealing then."

"How—?"

"Djaper is too clever for his own health, and you are not so stupid that you'd fail to reward yourself through his cleverness. Perhaps you decided stealing was too much trouble and killed Hormin instead."

"No!"

Abu spoke for the first time. "Let me take a cattle brand to him, lord. I'll make him confess."

"Merciful Amun," Imsety groaned.

"The whip is faster," said a charioteer. "No need to build a fire and heat the brand."

Meren held up a hand for silence. "Which do you prefer, Imsety, the whip or the brand?"

Imsety's face had turned the color of the whitewashed walls. He licked his lips. His mouth worked, but no words came.

"I have said the truth. Djaper told me the collar was the solution to all our troubles. It's so valuable. By the powers of Maat, goddess of truth, I have spoken no lies."

Meren rose. Folding his arms over his chest, he stared at his gilded sandal, then glanced at Imsety.

"You may go."

Imsety gaped at him.

"Go, fool."

A charioteer hauled Imsety to his feet and shoved him toward the door.

"Imsety."

Hormin's son turned back as Meren called to him.

"Think not of running away. I would find you, and then you would have both the whip and the brand."

Imsety dipped his head and trundled out of the hall to the accompaniment of the laughter of Meren's charioteers.

Meren snorted, then said to Abu, "His tale, it is proven?"

"Yes, lord. They spent some hours after the evening meal in the company of an assistant overseer of the Temple of Amunhotep III, then went to a beer house and shared a woman. The woman described both Djaper and Imsety. Imsety went first and then left the beerhouse. After that, either could have killed Hormin, or both."

"But first they robbed him."

"Yes, lord."

"Why rob him if they planned to kill him?" Meren asked himself.

None of his men answered. Rousing himself from his speculation, Meren noted the deep gold of the sunlight coming through the open door. The day was waning, and he had no answers to the murder of either Hormin or Bakwerner. He thought about paying another visit to Hormin's family, but he wanted to give Imsety plenty of time to alarm Djaper. Tomorrow morning he would descend upon them without warning.

Shadows fell across the threshold as his steward ushered in two visitors. Meren recognized the keeper of wills of the House of Life, Seb, who had held the post before Meren was born. Seb's dry, yellow-nailed hand rested for support on the shoulder of a youth round-eyed with excitement and curiosity. Meren accepted Seb's greeting and waved a hand. A charioteer brought a stool, and when Seb had settled on it, Meren resumed his stance, leaning against a column.

"You have brought the will of the scribe Hormin yourself, good Keeper."

"Don't I always when there's a good murder?" Seb asked with a cackle that ended in a cough. "Would have come sooner, lord, but this addled gander here had misfiled the original and we were a time hunting it down."

The youth, who had been devouring the weapons and gear of the charioteers, brought his gaze back to Meren and flushed. Having himself been embarrassed by his elders, Meren made no comment. He held out his hand to the youth. The boy gaped at it, then dove for the leather case slung over his shoulder, delved inside, and produced a roll of papyrus.

Meren broke the clay seal of the House of Life, unrolled the papyrus, and read. The room filled with the sound of Seb's labored breathing. Meren skimmed the list of possessions, then noted the half-dozen witnesses. Most were from the House of Life, including Seb, but old Ahmose's name was there as well. None of Hormin's family seemed to have signed; nor had Beltis. No doubt Hormin had kept his intentions to himself as a weapon.

Letting the will snap shut, he held it out. Abu took it from him.

Seb cackled again. "A grand design for cataclysm, is it not?"

"What do you know, you old gossip-monger?" Meren asked.

"Naught, lord. Naught of murder. I only know that this dead one, this Hormin, caught my interest. As you see, the will is only a few months old. Even so, I wouldn't have remembered it, or him, if he hadn't offended all my assistants by the time the will was ready for witnessing. That one, he ate and drank furor, survived on the animosity he created more than on the food he consumed. I knew he'd end up standing before the gods, done in violently."

Meren sighed, hardly surprised at the news. "Have you anything of substance to tell me, or have you come to pry knowledge of this murder from me?"

"An old man has few joys in life, my lord."

Seb was whining now, which meant he had come for gossip. Unfortunately, Meren would no doubt need his cooperation in the future. Reluctant to send him away unsatisfied, he spent much more time than he would have liked satisfying Seb's curiosity without giving away important details.

When the old man had gone Meren retreated with Abu to his office, where he reviewed the notes taken by his scribes. Abu read to him reports of inquiries to Hormin's neighbors and household.

"The maids of both Selket and the concubine swear their mistresses were at home asleep," the aide said. "They were pressed hard, and both remained adamant."

Meren pinched the bridge of his nose and laid aside a sheaf of notes. "Curse it, no witnesses to either murder, no witnesses who saw Hormin go to the Place of Anubis."

"But Bakwerner was seen lurking about Hormin's house several nights before the murder. A maid next door was entertaining a lover and saw him on two separate nights."

Nodding, Meren rose and stretched. "So Bakwerner could have been planning to kill Hormin, and finally did, but then who killed Bakwerner? And why?"

"Perhaps the young one, Djaper," Abu replied. "After

all, Bakwerner charged into his house bellowing that he 'knew things' and calling for Djaper's blood."

"Or Djaper could be the murderer, and Bakwerner his second victim. Curse it, Abu, I detest being in the midst of an abundance of possible killers."

"Aye, lord. Rarely have I seen a man so hated, or a collection in one place of so many capable of murder."

Meren smiled grimly at his aide. He was about to suggest dinner when a charioteer rapped on the door and entered.

"Well?" he snapped. His men knew him better than to disturb him when he was in one of his pondering sessions. There was news, and it was most likely bad.

"It is the concubine, lord. The concubine Beltis. She packed herself and her boy and left the house. She went to the village of the tomb makers after another quarrel with the family. You should have heard the screaming and howling."

"I have. Was there aught of interest among the screams and howls?"

"No, lord. Only the same accusations and threats. She only threw a few vases and pots this time. The old woman did kick her ass as she stomped out of the doorway, though." The charioteer grinned, evoking a smile from Meren.

"Gods, I would have liked to have seen that."

"Aye, my lord. It was a pleasing sight."

After dismissing Abu and the charioteer, Meren went to the house in search of food, though his appetite had waned. He knew the cause. Beltis had gone to the village of the tomb makers. Beltis was a dangerous woman, possibly a murderer, and like a spider she'd scrambled and scurried away from a place of exposure to make a nest and cast her web—much too near his son.

▽

9

Kysen stood on the roof of Thesh's house watching the horizon turn a deep turquoise, then ignite with a soft, creamy orange. Behind him stood several beds used by the household on hot nights. The one behind the wicker screen was his. Voices of women and their laughter came to him from open doorways and the street below as they worked to prepare the evening meal. He took a long sip of beer from a glazed cup. His first day in the tomb-makers' village was almost over, and he had yet to speak with the draftsman Woser. The beer turned sour in his stomach as he remembered going to Woser's house with Thesh.

The scribe had warned him of Woser's illness, which had been growing upon him for over a week and had worsened during the previous two days. Thesh attributed Woser's inability to keep food in his belly to his dissatisfaction with being a draftsman. Woser longed to become a sculptor, to the amusement of the whole village. Woser sculpted as if he were blind.

Kysen had insisted upon seeing Woser, but when Thesh conducted him down the main street past curious servants and artisans' wives, they could hear retching sounds from a house near the end of the road. Kysen exchanged glances with the scribe as they paused on the threshold of Woser's residence. Like most of the houses in the village, it consisted of four rectangular rooms running one behind the other.

Thesh stuck his head in the doorway. Beyond him Kysen could see a family common room strewn with cushions along one wall. High, narrow windows close to the ceiling let in little light, but he noticed a block of limestone in one corner around which were littered a sculptor's tools. Near the door lay a table, ink pots, pens, and sketches of a tomb shaft. He heard Thesh suck in his breath. The scribe drew back from the doorway abruptly, grimacing. Kysen glanced at him in surmise, only to clamp a hand over his nose and join Thesh in withdrawing several paces from the door.

"Hathor's tits," Thesh mumbled through the hands that covered his mouth and nose.

Kysen lowered his own hands, took a cautious sniff, and moved several steps farther away from the house. "Woser's sickness isn't only of the belly, it seems."

"I forgot," Thesh said. "His wife mentioned he hadn't been able to go far from his chamber stool yesterday. She had me check the calendar to see if it was an unlucky day, but I could find no evil signs. She says he's run afoul of a demon."

Kysen cocked his head to the side and listened to the renewed sounds of gagging and moaning issuing from Woser's house. Clearing his throat, he said to Thesh, "Perhaps if we wait until this evening, he will feel better."

"Yes, yes." Thesh nodded violently. "I expect a physician from the city this morning who will attend him. By this evening, yes."

They had quit the vicinity of Woser's house immediately. After that, Thesh had informed him that several of the artisans who dealt with Hormin were on duty in the Great Place, the Valley of the Kings, restoring the walls and interior of an old tomb of the last dynasty. And so it was that Kysen found himself in the resting place of Pharaohs, where the dead kings mediated between the forces of chaos and order.

Thesh brought him to the Great Place by the workmen's route over the cliffs that bordered western Thebes. The path arced into the royal valley down three stone steps bounded by a wall on one side and a guardpost on the other. Past the steps he entered the realm of the dead, guarded by the royal necropolis police, the *medjay*, and by the gods themselves. The valley held hundreds of royal tombs, but also, at its center, living huts and warehouses containing supplies for the workers such as food, pigments, copper chisels, and the oil and wicks used to light the interior of the tombs.

Once on the valley floor, Kysen beheld an array of V-shaped channels filled in part with flints and debris from the slopes above. Into the sides of these channels were cut entrance shafts to tombs. None of them were for the living god, Tutankhamun; the king was young and there was plenty of time in which to plan his house of eternity.

Kysen had spent the remainder of the day talking with four men who had dealt with Hormin in the making of his tomb, only to find that they had been in the Great Place on the night of the murder. The artisans worked in shifts, eating and sleeping in the huts in the center of the valley, guarded by the *medjay*. Of those who knew Hormin, only Thesh, Useramun, and Woser had been in the village two nights ago.

Shoving away from the wall on which he leaned, Kysen turned to find Thesh staring at him. In that fleeting moment he perceived apprehension, which enhanced the faint laugh lines at the corners of the scribe's eyes. Then the lines smoothed and Thesh smiled at him.

"Have you rested from the journey? The trip to the Great Place is arduous for those not accustomed to desert travel."

Kysen set his beer cup on the top of the wall and returned Thesh's smile. "Much rested, I thank you. And now I would see this master painter, Useramun."

"Before we go, I must tell you that Beltis has come back."

Concealing his surprise, Kysen glanced over his shoulder to the street below. He could see two serving women carrying a water jar between them, and several men returning to their homes for the evening. No Beltis.

"She came while you were washing," Thesh said. "If you hadn't been inside, you would have seen her procession. Beltis enters the village as if she were a princess appearing on a feast day."

"I will speak to her as well." Kysen passed Thesh on his way to the stairs that led from the roof to the street along the outside of the house.

Thesh followed him. "Do not be surprised if she finds you before you come to her."

"Why?" Kysen paused at the top of the stairs.

Cocking his head to the side, Thesh pursed his lips in the first sign of ill humor Kysen had seen in him.

"Beltis never allows a possible admirer to languish in the depravation of her presence."

A typical scribe's answer—delicate, circuitous, and nasty. Kysen grinned at Thesh.

"You would set me on my guard."

Thesh merely lifted a brow. It was all the answer Kysen was going to receive, so he turned and descended the stairs, stepping into the blackening shadows of the street. A long line of open doorways stretched before him. Wavering light from oil lamps offered some relief from the darkness. Thesh stepped to his side and gestured to a house opposite his own.

A few steps brought them into the bright glow issuing from the house. Kysen remembered little of Useramun except his brilliance as a painter. The older boy had always seemed to have his nose nudging the tip of a reed brush. The glow from the house increased as they approached. Kysen blinked and realized that Useramun had to have lit dozens of lamps to create such radiance. Thesh opened his mouth to call out a greeting, but Kysen put a hand on his forearm, silencing him. A querulous voice was speaking.

"You sent him away on purpose." The voice was young, and cracked with the strain of adolescence.

A second voice, lilting and low, answered. "Abjure me not, you petulant colt. The master painter of the temple of Ptah offered him a place. Was I to deny him the opportunity to work in so high a station?"

"You sent him away because he was my friend!"

The second voice chided softly. "By Hathor's tits, Geb, you've grown into a nagging bitch."

Kysen waited, but there was no retort. He glanced at Thesh and noted with amusement that the scribe's face had reddened. He released his hold, and Thesh called out a greeting. They were bidden to enter.

Stepping into the common room, Kysen squinted at the dazzling light. Whitewashed walls reflected brilliance, and on every one of them glowing scenes of wildlife and the countryside that turned the room into a fantasy. Kysen glimpsed a vignette of a reflection pool with the fish darting through azure waters. To his left waterfowl sprang from a marsh, startled into flight by a hunter armed with a throw stick. Every feather, every line was executed with vibrant mastery. Suddenly Kysen knew, without doubt, that he was in the presence

of unparalleled skill. Now he remembered more of
Useramun—even the master painters had held him in
awe.

A youth bowed to them and scuttled out of their way
to reveal a man who rose from a cushion set between
two of the myriad tall lampstands that cast daylike
brightness on the room. The man came forward, stop-
ping in front of Kysen, and chuckled. Goose bumps
formed on Kysen's arms. He'd heard such a laugh
before—one filled with concupiscent anticipation. He'd
heard it at court, among noblemen about whom his father took care to warn him. At once wary and intrigued,
Kysen felt a tension within his body he usually only felt
in the royal palace or in the manors of certain princes.
That chuckle came again, and before Thesh could speak
the man before Kysen stepped closer.

"The servant of the Eyes and Ears of Pharaoh, life,
prosperity, and health to thee." Useramun's gaze trailed
viscously over Kysen. "Especially health."

"Useramun!" Thesh hissed at his neighbor.

Never had Kysen been so grateful for Meren's
schooling in the ways of the imperial court. He mas-
tered the impulse to draw his dagger. He wasn't wearing
it anyway. Instead, he regarded the painter solemnly.
Though Useramun moved closer, so close that he could
feel the heat of the man's body, he remained where he
was. At the last moment, just as Kysen was losing the
battle with his control, Useramun veered around him,
circled, and came to rest in front of him again.

He was still far too close. Finally Kysen allowed
himself to react. He lifted his brows and widened his
eyes in an expression of disbelieving astonishment at
this trespass. He heard another soft laugh, and Useramun stepped back out of striking range.

Kysen's voice cut through the sound. "I give you leave to address me by name. I am Seth."

"Seth," Useramun murmured, "god of chaos and turbulence. Has the name given you restlessness? Are you of a perturbed and dissolute spirit, like your namesake?"

"Goat's dung!" Thesh loomed at the painter's side, spitting his words. "Curb that lewd tongue of yours before you invite the cane and the whip. This is a royal servant, not some guileless apprentice."

Useramun gave the scribe not a glance, but continued to examine Kysen as he would a sacrificial bull. Kysen stared back at the man, who was of an even height with him. The painter was one of those men whom the gods had filled to the brim with sensuality. High cheekbones drew one's gaze to his eyes, which burned like molten obsidian. His lower lip was fuller than the upper, giving his face an expression of readiness, of utter willingness.

Kysen fought the urge to curl his fingers into fists. The fool had deliberately taunted him, secure in the knowledge that his person was as beautiful as his paintings. He'd risked a beating, at the least. Perhaps he was as enamored of risk and danger as he was of attempted seduction.

Thesh was chattering to him. "And he isn't usually so insolent." The scribe glared at the painter, who was still staring at Kysen. "Beltis's arrival has discomposed him."

He'd had enough. Without preamble he snapped at the painter, "What were your doings of the last week? Begin with the five previous days."

Useramun's smile faltered, then, to Kysen's annoyance, appreciation of a different sort entered his gaze. The painter gestured to the cushions ranged behind him and called to his apprentice for beer. Kysen cut him off.

"Your answer." He dropped onto a red cushion opposite the painter while Thesh took one beside him.

"Five days," Useramun mused. "Five days. Hmmm. But I was in the Great Place five days ago, and then in the nobles'—" The painter stopped abruptly and glanced at Thesh. "There is much work to do on the tomb of the Great Father, the king's vizier Ay, and on the walls of the tomb of the old king, which is being restored even now. And then there is the tomb of the Princess Isis. The foreman of the gangs on these tombs will testify that I was with them."

He'd remembered that the artisans worked for wealthy patrons in addition to their regular work. However, the longer he was in the village, the more he realized that Thesh and his fellow artisans worked more for themselves than for the king. How could he have missed the significance?

The king was a strong youth who gave little thought as yet to his house of eternity. He had given his permission to a few of royal blood to commission tombs in the Valley of the Queens, where princes and royal women were buried. The artisans had much free time, and Thesh had filled it with lucrative commissions from the nobility that would surely displease the vizier were he to hear of them. And Hormin most likely had known this. Had the man threatened Thesh?

Private commissions obviously supplied the artisans with luxuries; Useramun's house was filled with soft and costly cushions, his beer excellent and served in faience drinking vessels of Egyptian blue. Kysen glanced at the painter's hands. They bore no telltale jewels, but he wore an armband of bronze inlaid with turquoise. He glanced from the armband to Useramun's now-wary face.

"And two days ago?"

"Ah, by then I was free from my shift and back here at home." Useramun gestured toward the piles of sketches strewn around the room. "As you can see, there is much work to be done before a scene is painted on a tomb wall. I could have done more work, but that sheep Woser is ill. His bowels, you know. And fighting with that wretch Hormin did him no good."

"So you were working here two days ago."

Useramun smiled and said gently, "Yes, servant of the Eyes of Pharaoh. Thesh has no doubt told you I was here when Hormin came the last time. As everyone else, I heard his battle with the concubine, our succulent Beltis, as I worked on a draft of a scene from *The Book of the Dead*. Geb was here as well, and another who has since gone. Later Hormin came to me to discuss work to be done once his tomb had been completely excavated."

"I would know the whole of it, Useramun." Kysen met the man's inviting gaze with growing annoyance. "At once."

Useramun sighed in pretended disappointment and leaned on a cushion. "He came to complain of the price of my paintings." He directed a glance over his shoulder at a lush depiction of himself beneath a grapevine. "The man had the soul of a goat and dared complain of the fees. He was lucky I'd considered touching my brush for him at all. The old king prized me above all other painters, as does the living god Tutankhamun, may he have life, health, and strength."

"And your response?" Kysen asked.

The corner of the painter's mouth twitched, but not in amusement. "I told him he could hire someone else and be damned to the netherworld."

He was leaving out much, Kysen could tell. The painter had been at ease in the beginning of his narrative, but now his body had gone stiff and his lips pressed together in a straight line. He could force Useramun to say more. But would it be the truth? The painter got his attention with another of those soft and unsuitable chuckles.

"You want to know where I was two nights ago," Useramun said quietly. "Like Thesh and poor Woser, I was here. We were all here, beautiful servant of the Eyes of Pharaoh. Even Geb."

For the first time since he'd begun to speak, Useramun glanced at his apprentice. The youth had settled in a shadowed corner in readiness to attend his master and guests. Geb flushed so darkly Kysen could see the stain on his cheeks despite the shadows. He folded his body in obeisance, touching his forehead to the floor, and muttered something about bringing fresh beer. At Useramun's nod, he vanished through a doorway to the back of the house. Kysen rose and thrust a staying hand at the painter and Thesh.

"You will remain here."

Before either man could protest, he followed Geb out of the room. He passed through another chamber, nearly stumbling over a large, low bed carved of gilded wood. The dim glint of gold surprised him, as did the width of the bed and the ornate, lion's-paw legs. He heard the clatter of pottery and entered the kitchen. Geb was lifting a beer jar from its stand. As Kysen approached, his grip slipped and the jar thunked back into the stand. The youth bit his lower lip, then ducked his head to Kysen.

"Is what your master says the truth?"

The boy nodded without speaking, quickly, as if he hoped his agreement might spare him Kysen's attention. Kysen regarded the youth speculatively. He was pleasing of appearance, with a roundness about the jaw and fragility of build that spoke of his meager years.

"How old are you?"

"Fifteen, master."

"Fifteen?"

"In a few months."

"Are you sure your master was here two nights ago, Geb?"

"Aye, he was here."

"How can you be sure?" Kysen asked, knowing the answer.

Geb licked his lips and whispered, "We were together." His gaze was on the floor, but he nodded toward the sleeping chamber. "In there. All night, and the same the next night."

Reciting a curse to himself, Kysen whispered back. "If you wish I can send you to Memphis, or to Heliopolis. I know the chief of artisans of Ra."

"Please, master, no."

"You would stay with him?"

All he got was a nod.

"If you should regret your decision—"

Geb lifted his head. His eyes glowed with an inner ferocity. "You have seen his work. It is incomparable, incomparable. Great men seek his favor. He has pleased Pharaoh, who has decreed that none other shall touch the walls of his tomb. And he has chosen me, *me*, to follow him. I would not leave him, master."

"Would you bear false witness for him?"

Geb turned and lifted the beer jar, cradling it against his chest, and directed a look at the sleeping chamber. "You're wrong, master. Though it does not appear so, what takes place in the room is supplication, not subjugation. Apprentice I may be, but my will is my own."

"And if he were threatened, this most skilled and pleasing of artisans, would you not defend him?"

Kysen watched the youth weigh the consequences of honesty.

"Aye, I would defend him," Geb said, "for he has much to teach me, and I want to learn it all."

Geb bowed to him. Kysen considered threatening him, but this boy was obsessed. He'd seen the inferno of artistic passion behind that humble demeanor. No doubt Geb had known from childhood what he wished to do, had craved the life of a painter. The desire for artistry possessed him, and nothing Kysen could say would deter him from pursuing his goal.

Preceding the boy, he headed for the common room. As he stepped into the chamber, he noticed that Thesh had backed himself against a wall behind a lampstand, his attention fastened on the center of the room. Kysen glanced at Useramun, who was standing there with his back to the newcomers. He turned and stepped aside, and revealed a woman.

Beltis. She could be no one but the concubine. Meren had been accurate in his description. She had long, muscled legs and a small head almost dwarfed by a black wig with strands of hair woven with copper beads. To disguise her weak chin, she painted her lips so that they distracted the observer. In spite of the lateness of the hour, when most people were at their evening meal, she had anointed herself and dressed elaborately. Her body had been oiled, her bare breasts rouged at the nipples, and she wore green-and-gold eyepaint.

"Seth, servant of the Eyes of Pharaoh," Useramun said. "This is Beltis, lately concubine to the scribe Hormin. Come, Bel, my adored one, and meet someone who will teach you not to be so vain. Meet someone whose beauty makes you look like a wash pot. Are we not blessed that someone rid us of that jackal Hormin and gave us this treasure instead?"

Kysen gaped at Useramun. Beltis gave the painter a look that would have shriveled the hide of a hippopotamus, then remembered her dignity. Gliding up to Kysen, she pressed her arms to her sides so that her breasts jutted forward. He caught a whiff of heavy perfume and wrinkled his nose as she bowed to him.

"Hail, Seth, servant of the Eyes of Pharaoh, Count Meren. Have you, like your lord, questions to ask of me?"

"Why are you here? My master won't like it that you left the house of Hormin."

Narrowing her eyes at his abruptness, the concubine replied, "I grew weary of quarreling with Selket and the others. Djaper hates me. This morning he threatened to take my inheritance away. He said he would have me barred from Hormin's will. I grew fearful, for I'm sure Djaper killed his father."

"You, of course, are innocent."

Beltis drew near, so that her breast almost touched his arm. "Of murdering Hormin, aye. In other things, no."

A shadow fell upon them. Kysen took a step back, but Useramun blocked his path. Silence fell as he glanced from the concubine to the painter. He felt the weight of both their stares—a gazelle faced with a pair of lions.

Useramun reached out and snaked his arm about Beltis's waist. Gazing steadily at Kysen, he said, "Beltis, my love, will you dine with us? I have missed you, and no doubt you're as hungry as I am. The beautiful servant of the Eyes of Pharaoh hungers as well."

Thesh shoved himself away from the wall he'd been hugging and snarled at the painter. "You fool."

Kysen almost shook his head but stopped before he disgraced himself by appearing as flustered as a tumescent youth.

"I bid you good evening," he said, and moved to pass around the pair to the door.

He heard a sigh and glanced over his shoulder as he stepped outside. Geb had joined Beltis and Useramun. All three were looking at him. As his gaze met Useramun's the painter dropped an arm over Geb and drew him back against his chest while he pulled Beltis closer. Kysen turned away without changing his expression, and stepped into the night. As Thesh joined him, he heard Useramun's mocking laughter bouncing off the painted walls of his house.

10

Meren woke without opening his eyes. There was no light against his eyelids. It must be dark still. He remained unmoving, breathing evenly, and waited. The click of the rings holding the curtains to the frame surrounding his bed had disturbed him immediately. Years of sleeping in the midst of campaigns against barbarians, years of going to bed knowing he could be attacked by a jealous courtier, these had made him a light sleeper.

There it was—that slightest of air movements. He rolled to the opposite side of the bed like a crocodile wrestling its prey, landed on all fours, and snatched a dagger from beneath the cushions. Shooting to his feet, he searched the darkness for the intruder.

"Well done," said an admiring young voice. "Karoya, put down that sword and go away. He's awake now, and yes, you were right to tell me to be wary."

Meren lowered his dagger and squinted in the darkness in the direction of the voice. "Majesty?"

Behind him he heard a click, and the flare of a lamp wick. Darkness receded as the king's giant Nubian bodyguard handed him the lamp. As the man vanished, Meren was left staring, his jaw slack, as the living god of Egypt grinned at him and sat on his bed. Tossing the dagger on the sheets, Meren knelt and bowed his head.

"Please, can't you leave ceremony aside?" Tutankhamun asked.

"I think not, majesty."

"It is my wish."

Meren lifted his head and gazed at the king. Tutankhamun had lost his air of daring and mischief and regained that weary, sad expression Meren had come to know well. He should have been more perceptive. Smiling at the king, he rose and sat on the edge of the bed.

"Were you my son, I would thrash you for risking your life in such a foolish manner. I could have killed you."

The king's bright laughter rewarded him for this transgression.

"I have been cursed with assessing the year's harvest for the entire kingdom. I've wrestled with figures for weeks without end." Tutankhamun sighed and pinched the bridge of his nose with thumb and forefinger. "The High Priest of Amun is cheating me as usual, and still expects me to give him electrum obelisks and limitless access to my granaries. You, however, have been free to visit possible murderers and go among vendors and merchants in the market. Free, Meren. And in return for this freedom, you must tell me all about the murder in the Place of Anubis."

The king emphasized his words with a jab to Meren's shoulder. Meren grinned back at him, all the while searching Tutankhamun's face. The king's eyes were large and, when unguarded, expressed his feelings as a bronze mirror reflects light. He could see in them now traces of a young lion bound in chains, a life-loving monkey sealed in a pyramid. Without further protest, he related all he had discovered to the king. Tutankhamun listened eagerly, then shook his head in wonder.

"I thought my family cursed with evil."

Meren said, "Hormin and his family aren't like most of us, majesty. Still, I have yet to find one of them more suspect than the others. The wife, the sons, the concubine, his coworkers—any of them had reason to kill Hormin. And then there are the tomb workers."

"The High Priest of Anubis has begged an audience," the king said. "No doubt he will complain to me about your lack of diligence in finding the killer and laying to rest the demons aroused by the crime."

"He's worried, majesty. Such a thing has never happened in the Place of Anubis."

"Aye, but I will still have to listen to him complain." The king paused, giving Meren a sidelong glance. "Um, there is another matter. There are—there are rumors of visitors to your house, Bedouin, Hittites, a bandit or two."

"The High Priest of Amun must have heard that you touched me."

The king's shoulders slumped. "I'm sorry. I know I must be circumspect, and I wouldn't endanger you, but sometimes—"

"He has spread rumors before, majesty."

Tutankhamun glanced at the portico, where darkness was fading into the gray light of dawn. "He still hates me for what my brother did. Akhenaten should never have tried to destroy Amun and the other gods. The high priest, he liked not living in obscurity and going hungry and having his priests killed." The king rose and rubbed his upper arms as if chilled, then met Meren's gaze. "He's beginning to see that I won't be guided like a blind donkey. Meren, I'm sure he had my brother killed."

At the desolation in the king's voice, Meren slid off the bed to stand beside him. Trying to ignore his own guilt, he dropped an arm about Tutankhamun's shoulders. Startled, the king looked up at him, then relaxed into the embrace. Akhenaten's death had robbed Meren forever of peace, but he could still ease Tutankhamun's suffering.

"Listen to me," Meren said. "Every day, every moment, in darkness or in light, my eyes are upon you. The servant who empties your chamber pot, the boy who holds your bow, the chamberlain who announces your guests, the guards who stand beside you, I know them all. Were I to question their loyalty, they would be dead."

The king's head dropped onto his shoulder for a moment. After a while the boy straightened, and Meren dropped his arm. The pyramid stone of guilt resting on his heart lifted. Tutankhamun held out his hand, and Meren grasped the boy's arm above the wrist, one warrior acknowledging another.

"It's just that I know how many enemies Pharaoh has," the king whispered. "There are so few I can trust. I wish my brother hadn't died."

"Majesty."

Meren couldn't help but wince, but the king hadn't seen or heard him. Meren could see that he was lost in old and sad memories.

"Majesty." This time the king looked at him. "For a long time now I have felt that I had two sons—Kysen, and you."

He bore Tutankhamun's searching gaze without apprehension, and at last the king smiled a genuine, carefree smile. It faded a little as he glanced at the growing light.

"I must go," the king said. "If anyone discovers that I've been here, you'll be in more danger than you are already. But you must come to me soon, for I'm anxious about this business in the Place of Anubis. After all my work restoring order to the kingdom, I won't have some criminal disturbing the harmony and balance of Egypt with this sacrilege."

Meren nodded gravely, suppressing a grin at the king's peremptory tone. Much as he longed for the freedom of boyhood, Tutankhamun understood governance in ways that eluded the many spitting vipers who called themselves his courtiers. Meren preceded the king through his house, taking care that they met none of his household who might have risen early. At the front gate he watched Tutankhamun slink down the street in the direction of the palace, Karoya at his side. The boy would steal over the palace walls with ease. Having trained the king himself, Meren could hardly complain if he used his skills now; he could only hope that Pharaoh's visit had been indeed secret.

Calling to his steward, he readied himself quickly for a visit to the house of Hormin. It was time to descend upon the family and frighten them, now, before they were fully awake. Taking with him several charioteers and his aide Abu, he burst upon his victims as they dined. Striding swiftly into the house, he came upon Imsety and his mother sharing a small table laden with beer and bread. Servants scurried out of his path when he crossed the threshold. Meren glared at Selket.

"Mistress, your sons are thieves, and most likely murderers."

Selket's mouth was full; she gulped, then choked. Imsety remained quiet and pounded his mother's back. Selket grabbed her cup and took several swallows. Gasping for breath, she shook her head.

"You deny my words," Meren said. He squeezed his eyes almost closed and stared at her. "Perhaps you have been behind this evil all along."

Imsety rose, causing his chair to tip backward and land on the floor. "No!"

Two charioteers brushed past Meren, drawing their scimitars. Imsety held his hands away from his body and stepped back a pace. At a word from Meren, the charioteers halted midway between their leader and Imsety.

"Please, lord, my sons are innocent." Selket had dropped to her knees.

Meren glanced about the room, then stalked out without a word. He remembered the way to Djaper's chamber. Thrusting the door aside, he charged into the room. At once he caught the stench. Behind him Abu sniffed and cursed. Meren felt his aide's hands on him. He was hefted bodily out of the chamber. Abu darted inside, weapon drawn. Meren prayed to Amun for patience while Abu searched the chamber, for he wouldn't be allowed to enter until his aide was convinced there was no threat to him.

"Enter, lord."

The chamber's high windows cast a vague and diffuse light. Opposite the door lay the bed, and on the bed, sprawled and still, lay Djaper. Beside the bed, a chamber pot had been removed from beneath its accompanying stool. Djaper had vomited in it.

Abu stood beside the bed. "He is cold, lord."

"Send for my physician and more men."

Meren examined the body. Its stiffness told him that Djaper had been dead at least several hours, but not longer than a day. He'd learned long ago that the body protested the passing of the *ka* in this manner, as though death had frightened it into rigidity. Eventually the muscles became flaccid, and he'd often wondered if this signaled the arrival of the soul to some place of shelter. Djaper's soul had not arrived, it seemed. He'd died sometime during the night—too suddenly and conveniently, before Meren could speak to him.

Glancing at the fouled chamber pot, Meren noted that Djaper had emptied his stomach. From the congealed state of the contents, he would guess this had happened before midnight. His attention was drawn to the floor beside the bed, where a glazed cup lay on its side next to a small amphora. He picked up the cup. It had been drained, and only a few drops of beer remained. Meren sniffed and wrinkled his nose. Not the best-quality beer. He lifted the amphora from its stand. As he did so, a clay seal dangling from twine brushed his fingers. He smelled the contents of the amphora. Half full, it contained the same tart beer left in the cup, but the bitter smell was stronger.

Meren dipped his finger in the beer and touched it to his tongue. Grimacing, he set the amphora down. As he stood, a wave of dizziness lapped over him, followed by a sensation of floating that caused him to sway. He hissed as he drew a deep breath. Stepping away from the bed, he braced himself by placing his palm against the nearest wall. He waited, chastising himself for his dangerous curiosity. Gradually his body returned to its normal state except for a strange lethargy and a feeling of elation.

Folding his arms over his chest, Meren gathered his wits, then surveyed the room. Little had changed since he'd last been in it. When he felt better, he lit a lamp and directed his gaze at the bed, the shelves of papyri, the chests. These he opened and found clothing, toiletries, jewelry. There was Djaper's scribe's kit, but he found nothing to indicate that the dead man had written anything.

Having searched the chamber, Meren returned to the room where Imscty and Selket were being held. Taking the master's chair, he regarded them silently. Imsety had relapsed into his habitual state of muteness. His mother, however, bit her lips in an apparent effort to contain her alarm and curiosity. She twisted her brown hands together unceasingly.

"Mistress, describe to me the happenings of yesterday and last night."

"My son, he asked to be left alone and keeps to his chamber still."

Meren didn't answer, and, given no choice, she went on. "Yesterday was like any other for me. I have the household to run, meals to supervise, weaving and mending, making of bread, ointments to prepare, the cleaning. The slut Beltis gave no help, as is her wont." Selket paused. Her gaze drifted away from Meren. "The concubine quarreled with Djaper."

"Explain."

"She invaded his chamber!" Selket's ire turned her brown face a ruddy hue. "She invaded his chamber yesterday morning, the harlot. He rejected her, and she screamed at him and clawed at his eyes. And she threw a bowl at him, which hit his head. Imsety and I came to see what has happening. Poor Djaper was on the floor holding his head, so Imsety grabbed Beltis and tossed her out of the room. She fled to her own chamber, and later she packed herself off to the village of the tomb makers. Poor Djaper had a headache for the rest of the day."

Meren snapped at Imsety, "What was the fight about?"

Imsety shrugged. "She'd found out about the broad collar yesterday. She wanted it."

"Eloquent as ever, Imsety. How did she discover it?"

"She climbed the palm outside Djaper's chamber and

spied on us when he told me to take it to the market for repairs."

"A sentence of over five words," Meren said. "You amaze me. So, you battled over the necklace. Then obviously she discovered that it was you and your brother who had robbed your father's office."

"She wanted the necklace," Imsety said reluctantly. "She claimed he gave it to her before he fetched her from the tomb-makers' village the last time."

"And was she telling the truth?"

Imsety glanced at his mother, whose color had returned to normal. She nodded stiffly.

"Aye, lord," Imsety said. "She came home dangling it from her fingers and was furious when Hormin took it from her to keep in his office."

"And later?" Meren asked.

Selket spoke up again. "Djaper went to the office of records and tithes while Imsety—"

"I know what happened to Imsety," Meren said.

"And that evening Djaper came home complaining of his head," Selket said. "When he spoke to Imsety and learned of your wrath, he became distraught. By nightfall he was so bothered by his head, he asked to be left alone and retired. Does his head still hurt?"

"Mother," Imsety said while staring at Meren, "Djaper should be here. Lord, where is my brother?"

"He's dead."

Imsety blinked at him as Meren darted glances from the man to his mother. Although her son remained quiet, Selket shook her head, turned, and tried to rush from the room. One of the charioteers caught her. Meren remained seated, keeping watch as the woman struggled and her voice rose to screams. The sound nearly destroyed his ears, and as she wailed Meren decided that his news had indeed been a surprise to her.

Imsety was still blinking at him when he returned his attention to the man. To Meren's disbelief, a tear appeared at the corner of one of Imsety's eyes and rolled down the side of his nose. He heard a choking sound. Stolid Imsety began to cry, his face crumpling and folding into grooves and troughs of grief. All the while he remained standing in front of Meren as if it mattered little where he was or in whose presence he wept.

Meren had a choice. He could believe that the mother and son possessed the ability to deceive him as far more experienced intriguers did not, or he could believe they hadn't known Djaper was dead and truly grieved. As he watched Selket collapse on the floor, tear at her hair, and wail while her son cried silently, he was struck with the contrast between their reactions today and the morning after Hormin's death. Djaper had been loved. Hormin had not.

Had the mother sacrificed one son to save the other from suspicion? Was he meant to believe that Djaper had taken his own life in remorse for his crime of patricide? Perhaps he'd frightened Imsety far more than he had realized, thus stampeding him into another crime.

Or perhaps, during his fight with Beltis, Djaper had threatened her with banishment again. He could easily imagine Djaper trying to suborn his father's will and casting Beltis out of the house forever. Still, if such had happened, he didn't think Beltis would have left the house with Djaper in residence. Unless she knew he wouldn't be living there much longer.

The physician arrived, out of breath and sweating. With him came his staff, whom he set to work reexamining the dead man's room and the rest of the house. Meren could do no more himself, so he returned home to send a message to Kysen; as he sat in his office penning it, Meren felt another twinge of apprehension.

The boy must be on his guard. He was much afraid that, having gone to the tomb-makers' village as his father's servant, Kysen was in even more danger than before. Beltis was there, and the artisans themselves hadn't been removed from suspicion. No doubt by the morning's end Kysen would have sent word of the results of his own inquiries.

How difficult would it be for a tomb maker to slip out of the village and make his way over the desert hills and across the river to Hormin's house? It could be done if one were desperate enough to take the risk. If one were forced to go in secret, hiding and skulking all the way, one might still reach the destination in an hour or two. The trip to the Place of Anubis could be made by foot in that amount of time as well, perhaps faster if one braved a night journey by skiff.

Meren laid aside his reed pen and blew on the ink forming his signature. He folded the paper, sealed it with clay, and impressed it with his signet ring. Calling for a messenger, he entrusted the letter to him, then sat back in his chair to resume his worrying.

Too many were dying. Hormin, Bakwerner, Djaper. He'd given orders for a close watch on Selket and Imsety. Most likely one of them was the murderer. Kysen was to watch Beltis closely as well. Now he wished he hadn't sent Kysen to the tomb-makers' village. Concerned as he was for Kysen, however, he must allow the boy to do his own work.

Meren reached across the table and grasped the obsidian embalming knife that had killed Hormin. Someone feared neither him nor the judgment of the gods. Anyone that desperate or that stupid was dangerous indeed. If he didn't solve this mystery soon, he would cause all of those suspect to be brought to him and examined without mercy until one of them confessed. He would have no choice, for the High Priest of Anubis would soon howl for vengeance and blood. His adversaries at court would begin to spread word that he no longer pursued Pharaoh's enemies with diligence. The moments passed, and as they did, the risks grew.

Rubbing his eyes with his fingertips, Meren lay the embalming knife aside and reached for the stack of papyri containing the summaries of the inquiry for the past few days. Somewhere among all the recordings was the knowledge sought. Somewhere.

11

Roused from slumber by a scream, Kysen bolted erect on the long cushion that served as his bed and jumped to his feet. The scream came again—an angry woman's scream.

Whirling around, Kysen looked over the rooftops of five houses to one of those with a childbirth arbor. Lamps lit and placed on the top of the walls illuminated shadowy figures moving about purposefully. Kysen's tension eased as he realized that the wife of the sculptor Ptahshedu had commenced her labor. He could see Yem entering the light structure of poles and green boughs erected for the birth.

Though it was still dark, the labor had stirred the village. He could hear children chattering and the splash of water as a servant poured jugs of it over someone in a bath stall. Beneath these sounds hissed the familiar scrape of grindstones as bread was prepared. The village was awake. Nevertheless, he found himself alone. Then he remembered.

After leaving Useramun and Beltis, he had decided to keep watch over the two from this roof. He'd feigned weariness to Thesh and Yem and retired to bed. Yem had been in a silently resentful mood, no doubt due to the arrival of Beltis. She'd ensconced herself on the cushions in the common room without addressing a word to her husband.

Thus Kysen had been alone several hours later when, from his rooftop concealment, he saw Thesh leave the house. Useramun's door was still open, but much less light issued from the interior of his house. Thesh stood in the middle of the street and stared at the painter's threshold, then turned. As he left, someone sidled out of the alley between Useramun's house and the next. Beltis.

She called to Thesh, who started, then whipped about as she caught his arm. Dragging the scribe to her, she sought the obscurity of the alley again. Kysen craned his neck and found her again as she thrust Thesh against a wall and pressed herself against him. Thesh tried to pry her from his body at first, then dove for the blackest shadows with the concubine in his arms. Kysen had listened, but heard nothing from them. He'd waited, drumming his fingers on the wall and surveying the street.

Eventually the two emerged. Thesh looked as flustered as a virgin, while Beltis resembled a sated cat. While the scribe returned to his own home, the concubine waited for him to close his door. When he was gone, she sauntered down the street. Kysen had been surprised when she stopped at Woser's house and mounted the stairs to the roof. Did the woman never sleep? And Woser ill. His thoughts upon Hormin's busy concubine, Kysen watched the women moving about the childbirth arbor, his hip resting on the wall top.

"You're awake."

Kysen spun around to face the object of his reverie. Beltis came toward him looking as rested as if she'd spent the night asleep, which he doubted. For the first time he regretted being unclothed before a woman. He should have slept in a kilt, or at least a loincloth.

"Does Yem know you're here?" he asked.

Beltis smirked. "I came up the outside stairs, and anyway, most of the women are busy with the labor."

She floated over to him and stood so close he could feel the heat of her body.

"You aren't like your master," she said.

He only stared at her.

"Have you caught the one who murdered Hormin?"

"Would I waste time here if we had?"

He quickly appraised his situation as she moved closer to him. She must have a low opinion of the intelligence of men to approach him so. Useramun, Thesh, Woser, Hormin. What was she about? He needed to know, and to find out he would have to refrain from spurning her. Kysen allowed himself to forget for a moment that she might be a murderer and let his gaze drift from her oiled and painted mouth down to her breasts, her thighs. The appraisal signaled an invitation to Beltis—and she accepted it.

The solar orb had risen by the time she left him. Exhausted, he dozed for a few moments while the village came fully to life. Soon Yem roused him for a meal of fresh bread and roasted fish. It was eaten in silence; Yem refused to speak to Thesh, who refused to speak to Yem. Kysen broke the stalemate by asking Thesh to conduct him once more to the house of the draftsman Woser.

Woser wasn't at home. Cursing himself for his slackness, Kysen interrogated the draftsman's mother and father only to find that Woser had improved miraculously upon receiving a visit from Beltis last night. Thanking the pair abruptly, he made for Beltis's home with Thesh in tow.

"Is there one man Beltis hasn't had?" Kysen snapped.

Thesh quickened his step to keep up with his guest.

"There are fewer who have received her favor than you think. Useramun, myself, Hormin, and—Woser . . ." The scribe frowned over this last name, then continued. "In this village at least, there are no more. By the gods, do you think she would have time for others?"

"Perhaps not."

Kysen added himself to Thesh's list as he strode toward Beltis's house. Someone called to them. Running down the street was a messenger clutching a folded papyrus. Kysen halted as the man reached him, accepted the letter, and noted the man's urgent gaze. Turning to Thesh, he smiled.

"I must consult with my master's man, if you would pardon me."

Thesh bowed and Kysen led the messenger down the street, through the gate, and beneath the scribe's pavilion. Under its shelter he received the news of Djaper's death.

"When?"

"Some time after the moon had set, lord. As I was leaving, the physician told the master that there was much essence of poppy in his beer."

"And no sign of who poisoned the beer."

Kysen sighed and removed a letter to his father from the waistband of his kilt. Entrusting it to the messenger, he dismissed the man. His father's letter had closed with a warning of danger. Given the constant comings and goings in the tomb-makers' village, one of the artisans could be responsible for Djaper's death. Even Thesh could have gone to Hormin's house in the middle of the night.

The object of his speculation emerged from the village and came to stand beside him. Kysen was contemplating sending for more men to question all the villagers at once when the scribe began to speak glumly.

"You have had news." Kysen nodded, but refused to enlighten Thesh, who went on. "Yem is furious. She says she will divorce me."

"I would," Kysen said.

Casting him a surprised glance, Thesh sighed. "I can't help myself. Beltis has such appetite. Her violence is like a fire in my body." Thesh groaned. "Yem will take all her property with her, and I owe her many copper *deben* from our marriage contract."

"Perhaps she will relent," Kysen said, laying a hand on the suffering man's shoulder. "Come, we must find Woser."

Thesh pointed in the direction of the path to the nobles' cemetery. "He is there."

Two people walked down the path from the nobles' cemetery—Beltis and a man. Beltis clung to the man's arm as if she was afraid to slip on the gravel. She and Woser drew nearer, and Kysen was able to see him more clearly.

The draftsman was one of those whose face was dominated by his nose. It jutted forth from his brow like the prow of one of Pharaoh's seagoing ships. Widening quickly, it became a brown, fleshy knob that almost obscured his mouth and chin. Shallow of chest, Woser was nonetheless tall, with stringy muscles kept toned by his use of sculptor's tools. His hair was chopped short and cut in a straight line across his forehead, which gave him a youthful appearance. Yet Kysen knew the draftsman was at least ten years older than himself.

To Kysen's amusement, the pair slowed as they recognized him. He was sure they would have avoided him if he hadn't beckoned to them as they came toward the gate. When they'd gained the pavilion, Beltis dropped

Woser's arm and smiled at Kysen and Thesh. No blush, no downcast eyes. Kysen frowned at the woman, who seemed amused at encountering three of her men at once. He could see no cause for mirth, and for the first time he glimpsed some of the humiliation many women endured as one of a collection of amusing objects. Kysen dragged his attention back to the pair in front of him as Thesh introduced him to Woser.

"You seem to have recovered quickly from your illness," Kysen said.

"Beltis brought a soothing potion from the city," Woser replied. "I am much improved."

"And I'm told you were cast down by this illness for many nights previously."

Woser's mouth drew down at the corners. There were lines about it, making it apparent that he often wore an expression of discontent.

"You're asking where I was when the scribe was killed. I was sick at home. Thesh will tell you how it is with me. No doubt my troubles are due to working in the Great Place on an unlucky day. I found out last week when Thesh showed me his calendar. I'm sure I was beset by a demon of the netherworld. After that day, I began to have trouble in my bowels. The demon was so powerful that none of the village cures worked. I prayed to Isis and Amun, to Bes, and even to Ptah."

Kysen jumped in before Woser could catch his breath and begin again. "Yes, yes. I've heard of your sufferings, but what took you to the nobles' cemetery so quickly after you regained your heath?"

"It was I." Beltis oozed over to stand beside him and gaze up into his eyes. "After my cure worked, I was anxious to see that the preparations for my lord's tomb were proceeding. I don't trust Djaper or Imsety to carry out their duty, despite Hormin's will." She smiled sweetly at Woser. "But to my surprise, the wall surfaces are complete. Everything will be ready by the time my lord is reawakened."

"And last night, both of you were here." Kysen's voice faded.

He hadn't really asked a question, for he already knew the answer. No doubt he'd find that Djaper had died after Beltis had arrived in the village and while Woser was still on his sickbed. He wouldn't reveal the death yet, for he still had to inquire into the movements of his other suspects.

As he dismissed the two, Thesh touched his arm. Glancing at the scribe, he followed the direction of his gaze to the point where the river path descended into the valley of the tomb makers. The daily supply train was winding its way down the path, and in its wake walked two men. Even at this distance he knew them. His brothers had returned.

Meren paced in his office. Swerving past a column in the shape of a papyrus bundle, he swept past the ebony chair on which his juggling balls lay and whirled when he reached the wall painted with a mural of his three daughters. The messenger had brought Kysen's report, reassurance that his son was safe. Still, Meren worried.

On his trip back past the ebony chair he scooped up his juggling balls. Tossing them in a circular pattern, he sent them high into the air, catching them and tossing them again in a furious burst of activity. When he'd first bought Kysen, he'd thought he wouldn't worry so much over a son as he had his daughters. Fool.

Hormin, Bakwerner, Djaper. Was there but one killer? If so, then Bakwerner and Djaper had been killed for what they knew—or what they pretended to know— about Hormin's death. Everything was connected to that first death. Hormin had been a creature of mediocre wits aided by sly dishonesty. According to old Ahmose, Hormin's talents hadn't measured up to the position he'd been chosen to fill. No doubt he had recognized his own mediocrity.

As his gaze traced the path of the flying balls, Meren realized that Hormin had suffered secret humiliation at the lack of an intelligent heart and had punished those around him for his disappointments and shortcomings. He resented his wife for hanging on to him when he no longer wanted her. He hated Bakwerner for rising in his profession when he was obviously even less able than Hormin himself. He begrudged his eldest son the farm he cared for so well and hated even more the younger for the intelligence and talent the gods had denied his father. The only person Hormin hadn't hated was Beltis, whose sexual skills were his as long as he provided well for her.

Meren slowed the pace of his juggling as he ordered his thoughts. Perhaps he would go to the Place of Anubis again. He also would confer once more with his physician about the poison used on Djaper. Then he would most likely summon the artisans mentioned by Kysen as well as Imsety and his mother and Beltis. He couldn't afford to wait any longer and risk another murder. The beatings would have to begin soon, if only to placate the powerful high priest of Anubis.

A knock caused him to grab his juggling balls as they fell and thrust them beneath one of the cushions piled in the corner of the room. He hurried to his ebony chair, seated himself in a negligent yet aristocratic manner, and called out his permission to enter.

To his surprise, Raneb the lector priest was ushered into the chamber. Marching up to Meren, Raneb glanced about the room curiously as he bowed.

"Most high and revered master, Eyes and Ears of Pharaoh, may the guardian of eternity, the lord of mysteries, the god Anubis protect you and guide your *ka*."

"He sent you to spy upon my progress, didn't he?"

Raneb was a thin, quick man whose narrow eyes and even narrower lips fostered his resemblance to a sand viper. Those narrow eyes popped open and rounded.

"No, Lord Meren, no. The Controller of the Mysteries knows nothing of my visit. No, I've come because you asked me to think upon the perfume that stained the dead man's kilt, and upon the heart amulet."

"Ah, then you're most welcome," Meren said as he inclined his head, giving Raneb permission to continue.

"I've thought and thought, lord. And I must say it's been hard since the sacrilege. The bandagers and the keepers of natron have been so skittish, chattering among themselves, whispering about evil spirits and the wrath of Anubis."

"Your point, priest."

"Oh, yes, um, the point. Yes, well, there is no point." Raneb hurried on when Meren scowled at him. "No point to the heart amulet, that is. It looks like all the rest we keep to place between the layers of bandages. No doubt it was spilled in the fight that killed this pestilence of a scribe."

Meren rose. "I've no time for self-importance, priest. You say the amulets are kept in a storeroom, not among the embalming tables. That amulet shouldn't have been in the shed. If you sought to call yourself to my attention in this way, you have, and you'll suffer for it."

"No!" Raneb skittered around to face Meren as he turned away. "No, lord, forgive me. I have never been in a murder before, and I've lost my wits. Perhaps one of us left the amulet in the shed by mistake. Not everyone is as careful as I, but I'm so troubled by this sacrilege. Perhaps that's why it took me so long to remember the unguent."

Meren leaned over the priest and snapped, "Unguent? The perfume on Hormin's kilt was unguent? Quickly."

"I'm an old man, lord, which is probably why I failed to remember the smell of this unguent. There are so many cosmetic salves, cheap and dear. Yet this one, this one is rare indeed."

Meren studied Raneb's bright eyes. "Rare or not, everyone uses unguents."

"Not this one, my lord. This is no common salve for peasants. *Qeres* is an unguent made of sweet resins and myrrh from a formula once known only by Pharaoh's perfume makers in the days of the pyramid builders. The recipe was handed down for hundreds of years. Its value would be beyond the reach of any but princes and great ones such as yourself."

"Curse it," Meren said. "There was nothing like it in Hormin's treasury hoard. Yet he got into some between the time he slept with the concubine and the moment he died."

"Yes, lord, but *qeres* is too valuable for one such as Hormin. One finds it only in the palace of Pharaoh, or the manor of a prince, or the temple of a god. I haven't seen *qeres* in many years. It was rare in my youth, for the instructions for making it were lost long ago and stores of the salve depleted. Even the wealthiest are no longer buried with a supply of it, as we of the Place of Anubis no longer possess any."

Meren nodded absently. Wandering back to his chair, he thanked the priest and lapsed into silence. Raneb bowed himself out of the room.

A rare unguent, a heart amulet, a scribe wealthier than he should have been. Had Hormin been a thief? Had he taken bribes in return for falsifying tax records?

He would send Abu to make inquiries. But the unguent—that inquiry he would pursue himself. If he wanted to know about cosmetic salves and perfumes, he could do no better than to seek the wisdom of the king's perfume makers in the royal workshops near the palace. His trip to the Place of Anubis and other plans would have to be delayed.

The Place of Anubis. What a bizarre place to frequent in the darkness. Few went to the Place of Anubis in daylight voluntarily. It was crowded with dead souls waiting for restoration to their bodies. It reeked of decay. The living deserted the Place of Anubis at night. Therefore, if Hormin went there, he must have had a reason of preeminence, a life-threatening reason or one that promised such reward that fear was a small price to pay.

In either instance, Hormin went in such haste that he hadn't bothered to change a kilt soiled by a rare unguent. The unguent, it was a sign, a mysterious one, as was the heart amulet and the broad collar. Like the connections between Hormin and his family and acquaintances, they were signs to be read. Like those wedge-shaped jottings the Babylonians used, they seemed indecipherable.

The unguent. He would need permission from the king to visit the royal workshops and question the chief perfume maker. He went to his bedchamber, readied himself for a call on the palace, and was at the doors to the king's audience chamber in less than an hour. He approached the royal guards in their bronze and leather corselets, only to pause. He'd been so preoccupied with the puzzle of the unguent that he hadn't paid attention to his surroundings. Abu and three of his charioteers had escorted him, but had fallen back as he neared the royal audience hall. Now he glanced about and noted the crowds of courtiers milling near the doors.

"Meren, you harem raider, you."

"General of the King's Armies, Horemheb," Meren said as he inclined his head at the armed warrior who emerged from a cluster of officials.

"I'll stomach no titles and piss-sweet courtesies from you. I've had a belly full of them today."

Meren studied Horemheb's scarred face and lowered his voice. "What's wrong?"

"I know not." Horemheb talked through a pained smile that wouldn't deceive a nursling. "We were listening to the delegation of the Mycenaean Sea Peoples when one of the king's personal servants sidled into the hall and peeked at his majesty from around a column. The king suddenly dismissed everyone, including the vizier, who is furious."

As Horemheb ended, the doors of the audience hall burst open and Pharaoh's overseer of the audience hall poked his head between them. He whispered to one of the giant Nubian guards. The guard, who like all of the king's war band revealed less emotion than a votive statue, merely raised an arm and pointed at Meren.

The overseer of the audience hall started as he caught sight of Meren, then pushed the doors open, came out, and shut them again. Rearranging his ankle-length formal linens, he cleared his throat and raised his voice so that he could speak in his accustomed boom.

"The living god, the justified, living in truth, Golden Horus, the divine one, son of Amun, King of Upper and Lower Egypt, Lord of the Two Lands, his majesty Nebkheprure Tutankhamun summons into his shining presence the prince, the Eyes and Ears of Pharaoh, Count Meren."

The doors, heavy with their enormous height and

laden with sheet gold, creaked on their hinges as they swung open again. Meren glanced at Horemheb in alarm. Pharaoh never behaved in haste during formal audiences. Divine majesty forbade such unseemliness. A chill settled over him, for a pharaoh had summoned him suddenly once before, and he'd been cast into horror. Abu made a quick movement as if to prevent him, but Meren glared at him, and he stepped aside.

Meren joined the overseer of the audience hall, who, despite his treasured dignity, grabbed Meren's arm and shoved him into the hall. Meren gawked at the overseer, who pushed him away from the doors and slammed them in his face. As they shut, Meren whirled around and put his back to them, expecting scimitars and daggers.

12

Meren pressed his back to the golden doors. His gaze met a sea of columns taller than the tallest trees, their electrum surfaces aglow with the light of thousands of tapers and candles in tall stands. He searched the shadows between the columns, but could see no one. At the end of the long hall, on a high dais, sat the golden throne of the king, but the living god wasn't on it. He was sitting on the last step of the dais, talking to an ancient man in a short wig and flowing robe. The old man was on his knees, whispering in the king's ear.

Tutankhamun shook his head, glanced at Meren, and waved the servant away. The man vanished through a door behind the dais. Meren walked swiftly to the king and knelt, touching his forehead to the floor. He could see a golden sandal.

"Rise," the king said.

Meren straightened. The king wore his formal robes. A cloth of the finest linen covered his head, fastened by the Uraeus diadem. His neck, arms, and legs were laden with gold and lapis and turquoise, but he'd laid aside on the throne the double scepters, the crook, and the flail. The high windows on one side of the audience chamber cast light on the king, and he gave off a glint like his father the sun.

Tutankhamun sighed and rubbed his temples. He almost smeared the heavy paint on his eyes. Abruptly he stood and walked away from the throne. Meren followed him until they were standing well away from the throne and some distance from any of the columns.

Catching Meren's arm, Tutankhamun pulled him close and spoke quietly. "Do you think they can hear me?"

"Who, majesty?"

"Anyone who's listening."

"No, majesty."

The king sighed again. He winced and rubbed his temple again. "She has betrayed me."

Meren felt his heart still. He stopped breathing.

"The queen?" he asked.

Tutankhamun nodded, studying Meren's face.

Meren became silent again. Ankhesenamun, daughter of the pharaoh Akhenaten, whose royal blood gave Tutankhamun one of his strongest claims to the throne. The girl had worshiped her fanatical, mad father. She'd never forgiven Tutankhamun for returning the kingdom to the old gods. Meren had never questioned Tutankhamun about her, for her relationship with her father had been close. Like her older sisters, she had been married to Akhenaten.

When he died, it had been Tutankhamun's duty to marry Ankhesenamun. Five years older than Tutankhamun, she had taken her elevation to Great Royal Wife as her due, yet hated her husband for what she saw as his betrayal. She had fought the restoration of the old gods, fought the return to Thebes from the upstart capital her father had built. All this she had done with a fanaticism and spite that rivaled her father's.

And now she had betrayed the king. She surrounded herself with zealots who had served her father in the old solar religion of the Aten. Had she betrayed the king with one of them? Or had she plotted an equally evil crime—the king's death?

Whatever the case, Tutankhamun had made a mistake in interrupting his audience. He was adept at intrigue, yet heartbreakingly precipitous when unnerved. His youth was the reason, and his youth endangered him.

"Sire," Meren said in as low a voice as possible, "how has she betrayed you?"

The king met his gaze, and he beheld the suppressed fury of outraged majesty. "She wrote to the Hittite king. The bitch wrote to my greatest enemy and offered to marry one of his sons if he would come and kill me."

"Merciful Isis."

Meren found his throat muscles thickening with tension. The Hittites rivaled Pharaoh in power. They nibbled away at the edges of the empire and fostered rebellion among the vassal states of Palestine and Syria. One day Egypt and the Hittites would go to war. If Ankhesenamun had succeeded, the war could have been brought upon them now, when Pharaoh was still a youth and ill-prepared to face the vicious multitudes of the Hittites.

"What am I to do?" The king drew his ceremonial gold dagger.

"You cannot kill her."

"She has committed the worst sin against me."

"She is the Great Royal Wife, daughter of a pharaoh. The kingdom has suffered strife and instability for too long, majesty. The execution of a queen will do great harm and shake the people's faith in you, no matter how innocent you are, or how strong."

Tutankhamun sheathed his dagger. His gold wristband and bracelets clattered with the violence of his movements. He lifted a tortured face to Meren.

"She hates me," he said. "She hates for me to touch

her—and she has endangered my people. I could forgive her for hating me, but not for the other."

"Nor should you, for either. What have you done?"

"Naught." The king waved his hand in a gesture of weariness. "I wanted to find her and kill her, but I did as you taught me and waited while I recited a prayer, then I sent for you."

"And Ay?"

"She's his granddaughter. He loves Ankhesenamun. I haven't the courage to tell him."

He noticed what was not said: that the king had discovered the queen's treason, not the vizier, not his eyes and ears. It was startling how well Tutankhamun had learned Meren's lessons in intrigue. Then he remembered the old servant. He was called Tiglith, a Syrian slave who had attended the royal children for longer than Meren had been alive. Tiglith served in the queen's palace.

"Majesty, you must continue your audiences."

"I know." The reply came out softly, belying the rage in the king's eyes.

"All of the queen's servants will have to be replaced, but we must avoid creating a stir in your golden hive of a court."

"I will give her a new palace."

Meren smiled grimly. "The one near the temple of Isis in Memphis?"

"Aye," the king said. "The high priest there detests her. The whole city hates her. And you, my friend, will supply the slaves and attendants. Set your people to the task at once."

Meren fell in step with the king and they paced back and forth in front of the throne.

"The arrangements will take time, majesty, and she

must be watched. May I have leave to—see to her majesty's comfort until she goes to Memphis?"

The king nodded, then halted abruptly and turned to Meren. "You should know I gave Tiglith certain orders. In the next few days Ankhesenamun will find herself growing more and more listless and unable to get enough sleep."

"Thy majesty possesses the wisdom of Toth." Meren hesitated, but the king's furrowed brow and lack of color spurred him on. "Perhaps word could be spread that Ankhesenamun believes herself with child and sent word to thy majesty at once. You were so overjoyed you were forced to dismiss everyone for fear of betraying your dignity. And now you will surround her majesty with the best physicians, the most careful of attendants, so that she and her child are cared for as befits the wife of the living god."

"I am such an attentive spouse."

"And I must be seen to go about my customary duties."

Distracted, the king's voice assumed its normal tone. "You've brought news?"

"Another death, Golden One. The son, Djaper, was poisoned yesterday or last night."

He summarized the events for the king and obtained permission to visit the royal workshops. Leaving Tutankhamun to deal with Ay, he quit the audience hall openly and made a show of obtaining a royal bodyguard who would gain him admittance to the workshops near the palace. As the Nubian marched ahead of him, he was joined by his own men. They walked beneath a succession of pylons and turned south, heading for a walled complex near the Nile. Once clear of the royal palace and its crowds of officials and courtiers, he spoke quietly to Abu, who fell back with two chariot-

eers and sauntered off in the direction of Meren's house
to begin arrangements for the queen.

Unable to do more at the moment, Meren resigned
himself to continuing with his original plans. He
mustn't show concern. Any disruption in his pursuit of
the murderer of the Place of Anubis would attract the
attention of those with evil intentions. Such attention
risked not only his life, but that of the king. The High
Priest of Amun maintained vigilance, ever watchful for
a weakness in the young Pharaoh. The Hittite ambassador would know of any disturbance at once, and seek
out its cause.

Thus he and his remaining charioteers went to the
royal workshops, passing easily by the posted sentries
at the gate. Long rows of workshops lay before him,
their awnings protecting the bent heads of jewelers,
sculptors, goldsmiths, weavers. He glanced briefly at a
shop where several men and women carved lapis lazuli,
carnelian, and agate for use in royal jewelry. At the intersection of the packed earth path with another, a procession of laborers bore supplies to a reed shelter where
scribes checked and recorded them and sent them on for
distribution to artisans.

The bodyguard stopped at a workshop that rivaled
Meren's house in size. Meren would have known what
it was from the smell of heated fats and spices issuing
from it. Before him lay a wide, open courtyard formed
by a low wall. Inside sat a line of domed ovens. Opposite them lay open fires and braziers tended by several
women. Two youths were stoking the ovens while a
third thrust a heavy pot of resin into one of them.
Meren followed the guard inside the workshop. He entered a room that resembled a small audience hall in
size.

Glancing at shelves bearing countless pots, vials, and

stoppered jars, he saw the guard address a man who resembled one of the ovoid jars on his shelves. The man hurriedly put aside a box of spice on a counter that ran the length of the room. He waddled over to Meren and dropped to his knees, wheezing. Presenting himself as Bakef, the king's master perfumer, the man touched his forehead to the floor. When he'd made his obeisance, the guard had to help him stand.

"It is my honor to serve and obey, mighty prince." Puff, puff, wheeze.

To Meren's questions about the unguent *qeres*, Bakef had no immediate reply. He fluttered his pudgy, pale hands.

"*Qeres, qeres.*"

Meren held out his hand, and a charioteer placed a scrap of cloth from Hormin's kilt in it. He tossed the scrap to Bakef. The perfumer snatched it and held it to his nose. Beads of sweat had formed on the tip of it. He sniffed again.

"Ah!"

Bakef fluttered the scrap, made a ponderous, belly-shifting turn, and waddled to a shelf. Retrieving a leather case, he pulled from it a sheaf of papyri bound by wooden stays. He leafed through page after page, starting in the middle. After a few moments, he poked a fat digit at a line of cursive hieroglyphs. Meren watched a gleam enter the man's eyes. The hillocks of his cheeks flushed as he reached high over his head and pulled a dusty roll of papyrus from a pile on the top shelf. He read the wooden tag attached to the roll and nodded. Sneezing, he brushed the roll, then wiped his hands on his kilt before spreading the paper and anchoring it.

Meren waited patiently, his attention only half on the perfumer, while he plotted a strategy to cope with the

Great Royal Wife. Bakef got his full attention when he suddenly clapped his hands together in excitement and rubbed them. He seemed to have forgotten his noble guest in his agitation, for he turned his back and trotted through a guarded door at the back of the workshop.

Meren followed him into a dim hall lined with five doors on each side. Ahead, Bakef had snatched up a taper and was muttering to himself.

"Ninth storeroom, tenth row, seventh shelf. Ninth storeroom, tenth row, seventh shelf. By the gods, the ninth storeroom. Who would have thought?"

Meren was right behind the perfumer by the time the man opened the fourth door on the right. Bakef touched the taper to a torch in a wall sconce beside the door. Yellow light illuminated a room crowded with shelves and made the faience and obsidian vials gleam. Jar after jar sat in neat lines—tall, cylindrical ones of deep Nile blue; squat ones of glassy black; bright yellow ones. Bakef picked up a stool in one hand and, with the taper in the other, wedged his bulk between the last two shelves at the back of the storeroom. Here the jars were covered with a fine layer of dust.

"My lord, I don't think I've ever had occasion to search the tenth shelf. I doubt if anyone has since my father's time."

Bakef set his stool on the floor and stood on it. Meren heard a crack and a snap. Bakef wavered and would have fallen onto the tenth shelf if Meren hadn't caught his arm. Pulling Bakef off the stool, he mounted it himself.

"What am I looking for, perfumer?"

Wiping his sweaty upper lip, Bakef ducked his head. "A jar of the finest alabaster. It should be shaped like a short, wide cylinder, and its top is decorated with a sculpture of a resting lion."

Meren searched the shelf. He found several vials and a big pot of dried herbs in an eggshell-thin pottery jar. He shoved this aside and glimpsed the pink tongue of a lion. Retrieving the jar, he walked back to the torch beside the door. He tried to lift the lid of the jar. It was stuck, and he had to twist it to get it open. The lid jerked free to reveal an interior empty of unguent.

All that remained was a faint smell of myrrh and a small piece of papyrus. Thrusting the jar into Bakef's hands, he read the notice that the last of the unguent had been used in the funeral equipage of the king's grandfather. One remaining jar should be found in the royal treasury.

Meren dropped the notice back in the jar. "He couldn't have gotten it from the royal treasury."

"My lord?"

Glancing at Bakef, Meren frowned. "Where else may this unguent be found?"

"Why, the only other notation I have for it is three jars housed in the treasury of the god Amun, may his name be praised for eternity."

"Ha!"

Bakef started and almost dropped the lion jar. "Is something wrong, lord?"

"He visited the treasury of the god on the day he died."

"The god died?" Bakef eyed Meren and shuffled away as if ready to bolt.

"No, you fool. Hormin died. But first the bastard visited the treasury of the god Amun." Whirling away from the perfumer, Meren strode from the storeroom without another word to the bewildered and wary Bakef.

The perfumer pattered after him, wheezing all the

way, and caught up as Meren emerged into the deepening shadows of late afternoon.

"My lord, I beg a word!"

Meren paused. "Well, man, speak quickly."

"If—if you find more *qeres*, and happen to come upon the recipe—that is—the queen—"

Meren hadn't been paying much heed to the perfumer. His gaze darted to the man's face, and he curled his lips into a sweet, benevolent smile.

"Yes, master perfumer, what is thy wish?"

"The queen sent word several months ago that she would like some *qeres*. I had forgotten, and the recipe is lost, you see."

"Did the Great Royal Wife say anything more of this unguent?"

"No, lord, only that a small amount came in some tribute from Byblos and was used up."

"I will see, perfumer."

Bakef stuttered his thanks as Meren walked away. The gratitude went unheard as Meren considered the meaning of this new connection between the murder of a common scribe and the Great Royal Wife. Was it a connection, or simply a happenstance? If the *qeres* on Hormin's kilt had come from the treasury of the god Amun, the unguent could still be that from the tribute of Byblos, for tribute was distributed among the temples of the gods as well as the royal household and favorites. Both the queen and Hormin might have gotten the *qeres* from the Byblos tribute. And Byblos was a known haven for the Syrian bandits who served the Hittite emperor.

Meren shook his head as he stood in the street before the perfumer's workshop. No, it could not be. As suspicious as he was, he couldn't imagine the low bureaucrat Hormin catching the interest of a Hittite spy, or the

Great Royal Wife. But perhaps he'd been suborned by the priesthood of Amun. Though for what purpose, even Meren was at a loss to understand.

And now he must make inquiries of the royal amulet maker and at the treasury of the god Amun. The business would distract him from the problem of Ankhesenamun. He would have to meet with the king and Ay, but he must do so in secret, after dark. There was just time after seeing the amulet maker to cross the river to the great temple complex of Amun before the evening meal. Then, when the city slept, he would go to the palace again.

13

The last cool breeze brought on by the setting of the sun whipped Kysen's hair back from his face as he watched the supply train plod toward them. A boy ran from the village to hand Thesh his scribe's kit.

The scribe swung the kit by its string. "Useramun told me that Hormin suddenly commissioned a coffin from Ramose and Hesire. Formerly he'd complained of the cost of their work. But then, he complained of everything."

Kysen felt locked inside pain, as though he existed somehow apart from the white valley, the noisy chatter of children around him as they spilled out of the village. He couldn't refuse to meet his brothers, not after Thesh's statement. Why was he afraid to do so? They hadn't recognized him before; they wouldn't now. And Pawero was still off at his lair, lurking there like some wrinkled old spider.

He and Thesh walked out to meet the supply train, and as they halted, one of his brothers separated from the line and came toward him. Odd to think that he wouldn't have known which was which without Thesh's guidance. The man stumbled, over nothing it seemed, righted himself, and then resumed his course. His steps were distorted, as though he were pulling his feet from

Nile mud, and he navigated like an overloaded freight boat with a torn sail.

Creasing his brow, Kysen said nothing as Hesire dropped anchor in front of him. The breeze carried gusts of beer fumes so strong they almost burned his nose. Ramose had followed his brother immediately, and joined them as Hesire drifted from side to side before Kysen on his drink-slackened tether. He raised an arm and pointed at Kysen.

"You," he said, sending a fresh puff of beer fumes wafting at Kysen. "I know you."

One of the first lessons he'd learned from Meren was never to give way to fear and spew forth ungoverned speech when confronted. Although his gut filled with molten bronze, he confined himself to two words.

"You do?"

Hesire, a man of lesser height whose jutting teeth and flabby muscles made him resemble a plucked duck, nodded and hiccuped. "Do. They say you're the servant of the Eyes and Ears of Pharaoh come to see about that bastard Hormin."

He jolted out of his fugue, although he pretended calm, and surveyed the line of hills behind his brothers. "You disliked Hormin."

" 'Course," Hesire said.

He set his legs apart to keep from drifting into his brother, folded his arms over his chest, and beamed at Kysen. Evidently he thought he'd made himself clear.

"Life and health to you," Ramose said, shouldering in front of Hesire. "I fear my brother has imbibed too early this morning."

Thesh glanced up from his place beneath the pavilion. "This morning and every morning."

Ramose scowled at the scribe, but continued. "Hesire

is furious with Hormin for getting killed before we could begin work on his coffin."

"Why? Surely you of all carpenters don't lack for commissions?"

Ramose glanced at Thesh, then fixed his gaze on his fingernails. "True, but Hormin commissioned a most complete and elegant coffin, and we prefer to make those. Three nested coffins, entirely illustrated with sacred texts and scenes from *The Book of What Is in the Underworld*. More challenging."

"I see."

He did see. It was as he'd suspected. Thesh was running a side business in funerary equipage, which was customary, but he and the artisans were keeping profits unknown to the royal authorities. No doubt many commissions such as Hormin's went unreported to the vizier's office.

Hesire belched and rubbed his hands on his wrinkled and dirty kilt. "And of course there was the sarcophagus."

"What sarcophagus?"

Kysen's skin prickled as Thesh froze in the act of recording grain supplies and Ramose tried to kill his brother with a mere gaze.

"What sarcophagus?"

"Why, that red granite one he's got in his cursed tomb."

"Hesire, you're drunk again," Ramose said.

He shoved his brother, who stumbled backward into a donkey and plummeted to the ground. Throwing up his hands in exasperation, Ramose hauled his brother upright and half carried him toward the village. Kysen watched them go. He didn't know whether he was unhappy or grateful that they hadn't recognized him. Glancing down, he found Thesh staring at him. He rubbed his chin with a forefinger, then shrugged, as though the significance of a red granite sarcophagus had eluded him.

While he watched Thesh record the distribution of supplies to the artisans' wives and take delivery on new chisels, hammers, awls, and reed brushes, he thought about how best to approach the scribe about the sarcophagus and the secret commissions. As he did so, Woser emerged from the village carrying a sack and a bottle.

The western hill beside the village was already beginning to bake in the unforgiving sun. Woser, a brown crane stalking up the slope, headed for one of the chapels cut into the hill. Beneath the chapels lay the tombs of the village ancestors. Kysen forgot Thesh. Surely Woser had fallen behind in his work after being sick. What was he doing traipsing off to his family chapel?

He waited for the draftsman to climb the staircase hewn out of the limestone. Low and wide, it had a central slide upon which funeral sledges were pushed up to the chapels. Woser turned right and stalked along a row of entrances until he came to the last one on the second level. Set into the hillside, it was constructed of mud brick in the shape of a steep-sided miniature pyramid.

Kysen watched the draftsman vanish inside before setting out to follow him. After climbing the stairs, he walked quietly to the tomb entrance and paused outside the open double doors. The chapel bricks, painted white, reflected heat at him. At first he could only see shadows. As his vision adjusted to the reduced light, he saw painted walls bearing scenes of deceased villagers receiving offerings from family members, of patron deities of the artisans. He slipped inside and placed his back to a wall.

The chapel had a short entrance hall that ended in

steps descending to the cramped devotional chamber below. He could hear Woser muttering there, and light from a lamp filtered up as well. Kysen walked halfway down the steps, paused, then descended until he could see the draftsman. Woser stood before an offering table. He was mumbling a prayer and holding bread and dried fish up in both hands. Then he placed the food on the altar, poured beer into a cup, and placed that on the altar.

Kysen was about to leave when he heard a snuffle. He paused, then turned back to stare at the draftsman. Woser wiped his generous nose on the back of his hand. He fumbled at the waistband of his kilt and drew forth a folded papyrus sheet.

Opening it, he began to read aloud. "O demon who hath tortured me for many days, I propitiate thee. Take this bread, this fish, this beer for thy sustenance."

Woser stuttered and sobbed. He wiped his face with the papyrus, then covered his eyes with the sheet and wailed incomprehensibly. He sank to his knees, rocked back and forth, and muttered into the papyrus.

Kysen drew nearer, hoping to make out what the draftsman was saying, but Woser suddenly coughed. Then he choked, grabbed the cup of beer, and downed it. Sighing, he folded the sheet and placed it on the offering table along with the food.

"O Ptah, O Hathor, O Amun, I beseech thee, make this demon fly from me. I mean no harm to anyone, not to the living or—or to th-the dead." Woser broke off to moan and rock again. When he regained some calm, he continued. "Make me skilled in drafting and in learning to sculpt, and intercede for me with Osiris and the gods of the underworld. I promise entire devotion. I never meant harm. I never meant evil. I beg to be delivered from sin, from this demon."

Kysen leaned against the chapel wall, disconcerted at the fearfulness in Woser's voice. Of course, if he'd been beset with such an evil illness for days on end, he might be fearful too. He thought Woser had finished, but he was wrong. The man stood, a papyrus reed with a nose, and began what Kysen recognized as a ritual exorcism. No doubt the physician from Thebes had recommended one as a part of Woser's recovery.

The draftsman produced a carved amulet, the Eye of Horus. Of limestone painted to resemble a stylized eye, it signified health. Woser lay the amulet on the offering table. Next he produced a pouch, took a pinch of the dust within, and sprinkled it over the flame of the oil lamp on the table. Light flamed, and Kysen sniffed the bitter smell of burnt herbs.

"Out, O demon. I call upon Horus and Seth, Amun and Mut, Isis and Hathor. Aid me. Depart, O demon. I have done no wrong. I have not killed; I have not spoken lies; I have not stolen. I am blameless of sin. Depart, O demon."

More chanting, more herbs. Then Woser produced another, smaller Eye of Horus amulet strung on a beaded chain, slipped it around his neck, and prayed. Kysen shook his head and stepped out into the open as Woser rose to leave. The draftsman started and gave a little cry.

"You cut short the ritual confession," Kysen said.

Woser's mouth worked open and closed.

"You left out quite a few sins." Kysen listed them on his fingers. "You have to say you haven't robbed the poor, caused pain, caused tears, made anyone suffer, damaged the offerings in temples, stolen the cakes of the dead or the loaves of the gods, cheated in the fields. There's lots more."

"What? Whatwhatwhatwhat?" Woser added for clarity, "What?"

"And you forgot lying with a strange woman."

Woser swallowed and gawked at Kysen.

"Tell me," Kysen said when it was apparent that Woser wasn't going to say anything, "has Beltis said anything to you about Hormin's death or his family?"

"Sh-she said his sons killed him."

"Many people could have killed him, including Beltis."

"I w-was sick."

"Yes, you appear to have been ill at the most convenient time."

"Thesh will tell you I—"

"I know, I know." Kysen turned toward the stairs. "Just remember. The Eyes and Ears of Pharaoh know much and discover all, eventually. If you know something about Beltis, you'd better tell me before I discover it myself and find out you knew all along. I don't like it when people withhold knowledge. Not at all. And my displeasure will make your demon's seem like rapture."

He left Woser then, knowing that a few hours of anticipating what might happen to him at Kysen's hands would work on the man's fantasy-ridden heart. When he emerged into sunlight, he saw that the supply party had dispersed. Thesh was leaving the pavilion with his arms loaded with packages and ostraca.

Kysen followed the scribe at a distance as he disappeared behind the village walls. He reached the gate as Thesh ducked inside his house. The man reappeared abruptly without his burdens. Kysen stepped quickly into the shadow of an unoccupied doorway and allowed several women to pass him.

Thesh dodged two girls playing ball in the street and walked directly into the house of Useramun. Instead of following, Kysen went to the side stairs that scaled to the roof of the painter's house. Climbing them, he slunk across the roof to the top-floor entrance and descended the ladder. He came out in the kitchen, where he encountered an old woman servant carrying bread in a basket. His hand went to his lips, signaling silence. She regarded him without much curiosity before quitting the house through the rear door. He crept toward the front room, lured by the sound of Useramun's voice.

"I tell you it means nothing," the painter was saying.

He was sitting before a grinding stone and spooning crushed red ocher into a pot. Thesh walked back and forth in front of him tugging at a length of black hair.

"You didn't see Seth's face when Hesire confronted him. He went pale. I'm sure he understood. He's got a most clever heart, that one."

"Aye," Useramun purred. "Most clever, and a fit body too. Perfect to the canon of proportions."

"Are you listening? He knows!"

"Shoulders broader than the length from elbow to fingertip," the painter murmured as he allowed ocher to spill from his spoon.

"If Ramose hadn't stopped him, he'd have mentioned the payments."

"Nose not too long. Lips soft, yet firm."

"And now he's following Woser," Thesh said. "Woser, with his demons and his sickness. Who can tell what Woser will say?"

"He has legs of the most precise musculature."

Thesh stopped before the painter, chest heaving. "Useramun, shut up and help me think. What if Seth reports what he's learned about us to the Eyes and Ears of Pharaoh?"

The painter expelled an irritated sigh and laid his spoon aside.

"Listen to me. Seth is a royal servant. We are royal servants. Royal servants know about side commissions and private arrangements that ease the conduct of royal business."

"You mean bribes," Thesh said as he raked his hands through his hair.

The painter cocked his head to the side. "Don't you think our Seth indulges in bribes?"

"No."

"Well, you're wrong."

"How would you know?" Thesh snapped.

"I asked Beltis," Useramun said. "The little bitch is already busy ingratiating herself with the servant of the Eyes of Pharaoh. She ingratiated herself only a few hours ago. Several times."

Kysen swore at Useramun silently while Thesh swore at him aloud.

"No use blaming me," the painter said as he took up his spoon again.

"But he's sure to suspect you and me now!"

"Why?"

"Because of Beltis, you fool. She's trying to bribe him with her body, and he's going to think she murdered Hormin and that we helped, or that we did it for her, or that we urged her to do it for us, or—what if she tells him we did it?"

"Gods, Thesh, you're babbling like a runaway slave under torture. Next you'll be soiling your kilt. He hasn't done anything yet. Nor has he said anything. Wait."

Thesh groaned. "But I didn't kill Hormin."

"I didn't either. And I don't think Beltis did, for I'm sure she wouldn't risk her oiled and perfumed hide to do it. Therefore we've nothing to worry about."

"No? What if they don't find the killer?"

Useramun shrugged and began to pour resin into the pot of ocher.

"What if they don't find the killer? What if the vizier becomes impatient? What if he applies pressure to the Eyes of Pharaoh? What if they decide to find the killer by torturing us? What if they decide to find someone to blame even if they're not sure I'm guilty? I could be cast out into the desert to die."

Thesh began to pace up and down again, this time working his fists open and closed. Useramun glanced up after he'd finished. Kysen noted the first sign of interest from the painter. Useramun chewed on the end of his spoon.

"Perhaps you're right." He chewed thoughtfully while Thesh paced. "Perhaps there is reason to take a hand in this investigation ourselves."

"How?"

"I don't know right now. I shall think upon it. After all, Beltis says Hormin's sons killed him. They say she did it. There seems to be an abundance of persons upon whom the authorities may place blame. It may be in our interest to see that they place it upon the right person."

"And quickly," Thesh said.

Useramun chuckled. "You mean before you deteriorate into a quivering mud cake?"

"No, before Seth confronts me about our commissions and the vizier comes down upon us with his wrath."

"Don't be an ass," the painter said.

"If I'm discovered, I won't endure punishment alone."

Useramun rose and traced Thesh's chin with the end of the spoon. "Then we'll have to find a killer for Seth, won't we? That should take his thoughts from secret commissions and bribes and other such inconvenient things."

Thesh jerked his head out of range of the spoon and went to the front door. "We haven't much time."

"Give me a day," the painter said.

"Only if Seth says nothing."

Useramun nodded.

"If he confronts me, I must throw myself on his mercy and beg his discretion, for all of us."

The painter had returned to his mixing, and he glanced up from the pot. "I'm sure you're very good at begging. But I think you'll be surprised at how unimportant our little doings are in the view of a servant of a great one. No doubt he's seen much bigger thieves than us."

Kysen nearly laughed. He had indeed. Thesh left vowing to confess all if cornered, and Useramun continued with his paint mixing. Kysen left the way he'd come. He managed to creep downstairs without anyone seeing him except for a plump little boy who could barely walk. The young one had wobbled down the alley between Useramun's house and his neighbor's and had set his bare bottom on the lowest step in the staircase. He was playing with a rattle.

Poor Thesh. All his charm and pleasing looks meant naught when he was confronted with—. Kysen stopped on the middle step and gazed at the boy below without seeing him. Useramun and Beltis; Woser and Beltis; Hormin and Beltis. And, of course, himself and Beltis.

He spoke aloud to himself. "Thesh and Beltis."

He took another step down as he mused. He nearly stumbled as enlightenment burst upon him. He stood still, pondering. Could he be right? How could he be sure? He considered the possibilities as he resumed his descent.

Kysen picked the little boy up as he reached the bottom step. "Aren't you Yem's nephew, little one? Come along. Let's see if we can't cheer your Uncle Thesh. He's got quite a lot of heavy burdens on his heart today."

14

Meren walked into the forecourt of the amulet-makers' workshop and paused to adjust to the clatter and pounding that assaulted his ears. Under the shade of an awning sat rows of apprentices and masters working with thin copper chisels and wooden hammers or polishing stones. Beneath each workplace lay a mat to catch flakes of carnelian, lapis lazuli, and turquoise. Beyond, in the open air, lay a fire pit and molds. Two men bent over the pit holding flexible wooden tongs. They gripped a crucible and lowered it into the pit.

An old man stood beside a balance laden with several pieces of lapis lazuli. When he saw Meren, he motioned to a younger man, who took up watch beside the balance. Shuffling up to Meren, he bowed low.

"Life, health, and strength to my lord Meren."

"I didn't think you'd remember me, Nebi."

"One remembers the Eyes and Ears of Pharaoh."

Meren rolled his eyes. "Please, Nebi. I used to hide from my tutor in your workshop."

Nebi laughed and placed a dry, scarred finger beside his nose. "Long, long ago."

"Not so long, I pray. But Nebi, I've come on an errand."

"Allow me to offer refreshment and shade, my lord."

Nebi ushered him inside the workshop past more

rows of assistants sitting on the floor or bent over work-tables. One was inserting glass inlay into a gold scarab amulet. At the rear of the shop lay a narrow room with a chair, a bed, and stools. Given Nebi's advancing years, he wasn't surprised at their presence.

"No," he said when Nebi offered the only chair. "If you remember me so clearly, then you know I'm not going to take your chair when you need it."

He waited while Nebi engaged in the slow process of lowering himself into the chair. Then he took a stool beside it and produced the heart amulet found on Hormin.

"What can you tell me of this?"

Nebi took the amulet. The craftsman had small hands for a man. No doubt they were an advantage in his delicate work. Each finger bore its net of scars and nicks. The carnelian heart with its smoothly worked surface made Nebi's hands seem all the more disfigured. He turned it over, brought it close to his face to peer at it, then glanced at Meren.

"The *ib* amulet. Couldn't they tell you about it in the Place of Anubis?"

"How do you know it comes from the Place of Anubis?"

"How do I know Ra is in his sun boat?" Nebi shrugged. "Such things are known. That is all."

Meren gave up. "Very well. I should have known better than to expect secrecy. Raneb the lector priest says it's one of thousands they put in the wrappings. I want to know if there's anything special about this amulet."

Nebi turned the object over in his hand. Formed in the shape of a stylized human heart, the *ib* resembled an elongated pot with double handles and a pronounced rim.

"This one?" Nebi's hand drew closer to his face again as he mused. "The heart, seat of intelligence and emotion. This amulet must be placed on the body during ritual purification and embalming to protect the heart so that it can be weighed on the balance of the gods against the feather of truth. Anubis stands by to assure the fairness of the weighing. I've often wondered how many of us, so laden with sins, ever pass the trial."

Meren shifted on the stool. "Please, Nebi."

"Yes, my lord." The old man handed the amulet to Meren. "The stone is of extremely good quality, most likely from a large pebble from the eastern desert. Such large pebbles are rare, as is the excellent blood-red color. Raneb may see many amulets, but he obviously doesn't look at them as a craftsman does."

"Well, they have great boxes full of them."

"Indeed, my lord. But this carnelian is of the quality I would use only in an amulet made for a noble or a prince or—"

"Or a king?"

Nebi inclined his head. "I am a *neshdy*, worker of precious stones." Nebi pointed at the amulet in Meren's hand. "That is the amulet of a prince."

"I feared you would say so."

"It's not pierced," Nebi said. "Therefore it wasn't meant for a necklace. It has been shaped on both sides. Therefore it is not meant for inlay. I would say it was intended to be placed upon a body, within the bandages over the heart."

"Therefore, if this amulet came from the Place of Anubis, it would have been housed in their treasury at the temple, not at the embalming sheds."

"Aye, my lord. But, of course, someone could have made a mistake and placed it with the lesser stones. They seem to take such amulets for granted, the embalmer priests."

Meren stood and helped Nebi get himself out of his

chair. They walked out of the workshop, back into the din of the forecourt. Bow drills whirred and blowpipes hissed as assistants blew into them to fan the furnaces and braziers. Meren took leave of Nebi and returned to his chariot. Abu awaited him, but he stood caressing the nose of his thoroughbred while he thought.

Another object of great value, this heart amulet. Did it belong to Hormin, or to the Place of Anubis? He was reluctant to admit that he might never know. Hormin had been prosperous, mostly because he hoarded and no doubt connived in sly ways to obtain more than his fair share of wealth. The scribe had owned that broad collar. Yet he couldn't make the mistake of assuming he also owned the unguent and the heart amulet.

"Abu, we're going to the treasury of the god Amun." Meren glanced at the sun. It had already sailed over its high point and was descending rapidly. "Who do you see at the treasury?"

"A lowly Pure One, my lord."

"It's as well. In that ants' nest the powerful ones wouldn't know anything of our Hormin. Not that they would tell me if they did."

He sailed across the river on the royal ferry, taking his chariot with him. Soon he was driving down the great processional way lined with ram-headed sphinxes, the pylon gates looming larger and larger until they dwarfed even the largest of the temples of the lesser gods. Gold-and-electrum-cased obelisks glowed in sunlight. Crowds of priests and temple servants, suppli-cants, and officials made way for him.

Meren craned his neck back until he could see the flagpoles with their narrow banners hanging limply in the stillness of the fading day. He hadn't been to the temple of Amun often since the court had returned from the heretic's capital. Each time he did, he felt as if he should wear armor and watch for cobras in dark corners. The High Priest of Amun disliked him almost as much as he hated the king.

Abu, who drove the chariot, walked the horses beneath the monumental pylons. The closer they came to the temple, the more priests they encountered—richly dressed in the whitest linens and in electrum and precious stones. Those of higher rank, mostly noblemen in gleaming, bejeweled raiment, advanced upon their way with the aid of several fan-bearing servitors. Weaving obsequiously through the numerous gemlike processions were the ordinary priests, the Pure Ones, who conducted the everyday affairs of the temple, such as providing food for the bureaucracy and teaching boys in the temple school.

Abu left the chariot in care of the temple guards who had greeted them and allowed them to pass with salutes. Inside the temple walls Meren skirted the temple of Khons, son of Amun, and crossed several courts to a long, vaulted building to the rear of the sacred lake. Beyond the lake lay the temple itself, shrouded in its protective curtain of stone and precious metal. Passing the sentries who flanked the double doors of the treasury, Meren walked into the antechamber of the building. He was about to ask Abu to find the priest they sought when he heard his name spoken quietly from the shadows of a recess that held a votive statue of the king's father, Amunhotep the Magnificent.

"Meren, dear cousin. You really shouldn't be here."

It was always the same. He turned abruptly, and felt as if he were looking into the polished bronze surface of a mirror. He faced a man who looked more charioteer than priest—tall, lean, and taut about the shoulders and legs, as though he spent most of his time in the exercise yard rather than the temple. Yet this man wore a finely spun linen overrobe that crossed over his shoulders in pleats and hung to his ankles and a heavy square pectoral necklace bearing the figure of Amun in electrum and turquoise. Heavy wristbands of the same materials matched the bracelets on his ankles.

"Greetings, Ebana."

His cousin leaned on one wall of the niche and gave him one of those priestly smiles from beneath a long, elaborately plaited wig. Meren had been there when Ebana began to practice priestly demeanor. He had been eleven and his çousin but a year older. A glance at Abu caused the charioteer to fade away in search of the Pure One. Meren approached Ebana, who hadn't moved.

When he was close enough to speak without others overhearing, he said, "I haven't seen you at court."

Ebana studied Meren quietly for a few moments. "I thought our resemblance would fade with the years, but we still look as if we shared the same womb."

"People know our differences."

"By the good god Amun, are there differences?" Ebana turned his head so that Meren could see more clearly the scar that ran from his temple, across his left cheek, and down his neck.

Meren shook his head. "I tried to warn you that night."

"So you say, but still Akhenaten set his minions upon me when I was in my bed, sleeping."

"We've rowed upstream like this too many times," Meren şaid. He sighed and threw out his hands in supplication. "I have sworn on my *ka*. I've begged you to believe me. Why can't you—"

"Why can't I believe you?" Ebana thrust himself away from the wall and stuck his face close to Meren's. "Bloody gods, cousin. Perhaps it's because I saw my wife and son die that night. No, too light a reason. Perhaps it's because I spent a few endless nights having my ribs broken. No, I have it. I can't believe you because I'm stupid. Yes, that's it."

Meren placed his hand on the folds of Ebana's robe where they crossed over his chest and gently shoved him.

Ebana allowed himself to be moved, but whispered violently as he crossed his arms and gave Meren another of his beatific smiles. "The only reason you're still alive, dear cousin, is because you interceded for me with the young king."

"All I want is peace between us."

"I'm a Servant of the God, dear cousin," Ebana hissed. "I am one of the few who may perform the secret Rite of the House of the Morning. I am privileged to enter the sanctuary of the god Amun. And I remember how it was while you wallowed in perverse sin in the heretic's court—priests and their families cast out and starving, their retainers and slaves and the workmen who depended upon their patronage, all starving. Weeds grew in the forecourt of the sanctuary. Weeds! So don't ask me for peace, Meren. You won't get it."

Ebana whirled away from him and stalked down the corridor, his white robes fluttering out to reveal the kilt he wore beneath the transparent garment. Meren clamped his will down on old memories and renewed grief. He must find Abu before word spread to the High Priest that he was inside the temple walls.

The treasury consisted of a series of long, narrow rooms flanking a central hall. Each room had only one entrance and no windows. Guards lined the hall and the columned entry foyer beyond the antechamber. Abu appeared in the foyer, ushering a priest.

Shaven head gleaming, his steps dragging, the priest stalled beside a column. Meren watched as the priest muttered to Abu, his hands waving frantically. He shook his head until Meren feared he would make himself dizzy, then scrambled back inside the treasury.

Abu returned to Meren and they went outside without speaking. Once submerged in the crowds of temple servants and priests, Abu gave Meren a rueful glance.

"He saw you with Lord Ebana."

"And he didn't want to be seen talking to me," Meren said.

"His superior, you see."

Meren stopped walking, and the crowd surged around them. "Your Pure One serves under Ebana?"

"Aye, my lord, for the past three weeks."

Meren began to walk again. The Pure One who had received Hormin the day before he died served under Ebana.

"And the *qeres*?" Meren asked.

"Hormin delivered tax-concession documents to the Pure One at the treasury workroom behind the vaults. The Pure One says that he didn't notice what Hormin did afterward because he was busy reviewing the documents. All he remembers is that Hormin wandered into the vaults and was thrown out by the guards before he could go three steps."

"He's certain Hormin got no farther, not anywhere near the vault containing the *qeres*?"

"We visited the one where the unguent is housed. None is missing, although one of the jars is half empty. They use it in the Rite of the House of the Morning when the god is fed and dressed."

"And my cousin is a Servant of the God, who may perform this rite."

Abu said nothing as they approached the chariot.

Meren glanced back at the temple complex. The setting sun turned painted and gold-covered surfaces into yellow fire. He knew that the brightness without contrasted with the cool blackness inside the sanctuary. The temple still bore scars where Akhenaten's soldiers and heretic priests had gouged out the names of Amun and any other god but the Aten.

Ebana wasn't the only priest who couldn't forgive. The High Priest and his allies, they could be behind the queen's latest treason. If it could be proved that she'd tried to bring the detested Hittites to the throne, the king would suffer, perhaps lose power to the priesthood of Amun.

As they drove toward the riverbank, Meren examined the possibility that somehow Hormin had been linked to the priests and to the queen. Yet however much he disliked the coincidence of the unguent, he couldn't bring himself to believe that so lowly an official as Hormin could be of use to either the queen or Ebana. He would have to learn more to be certain.

By the time he returned home, he was weary. He'd spent the day searching for details, had obtained them, and yet felt no nearer a solution to this murder. He felt as if he'd dropped a faience vessel and tried to put it back together, only to discover none of the pieces fit.

He discussed the reassignment of the queen's servants with Abu. Then Remi insisted upon a game of hunt-the-lion, so it was dark by the time he'd sent the boy to bed and had his own evening meal. Meren summoned his body servants and tried to take his thoughts from the murder by indulging in a shower. As a woman poured water over his shoulders in the bathing chamber, he deliberately thought of the letter from his eldest daughter, Tefnut, that had cheered him. It had been waiting for him when he came home.

She expected a child in the winter. At last. A child of his oldest child. Perhaps now Tefnut wouldn't resent

Kysen so much. He'd tried to explain to her about sons, but she'd been so young when he'd brought Kysen home. Now Bener, the middle one, she had liked Kysen at once, for he climbed palm trees with her and stole dates and pomegranates for her. And the youngest, Isis, had never felt threatened by a son, for she assumed that everyone loved her, and they usually did.

He donned a kilt and robe and went to his office to receive a report from the men watching Imsety and his mother. One of the men on duty still hadn't reported, although he'd been due to arrive since sunset. Annoyed at the delay, Meren sent a messenger before settling down to some serious juggling. He bolted the door to his office and rummaged in a cedar and ivory box set in a niche in the wall. He withdrew four balls of stuffed leather decorated with gold and silver gilding—his newest set.

If he didn't juggle, he wouldn't be able to allow his mind to rest. The only way he was going to solve this mystery was to permit his thoughts to germinate like barley seeds. Trying to juggle with four balls instead of three would require the concentration of his entire heart. He'd consulted with the royal jugglers in secret, and knew he had to keep two balls juggled in only one hand. He grasped a pair in each hand.

Sending the balls in his right hand bouncing, he tossed and caught, tossed and caught. Then he began all over again with his left. After a while he tried it with both hands at once, and dropped all of them. Then he remembered to stagger his start as the jugglers had instructed, and began again. He'd just managed to juggle two balls in each hand without dropping them when he heard someone running outside.

A gilded ball bounced off his nose. "Curse it."

He grabbed the balls and threw them into the cedar

casket. As the steps neared his door, he opened it. Abu saluted carelessly and gulped in a deep breath.

"Lord, they're gone."

"Imsety and the woman?" Meren barely noticed Abu's confirmation. Wrath snaked into his belly. "How!"

"I'm not sure, lord, but the guards are—they're—"

"Say it, damn you." Meren braced himself for what he might hear.

"They're sleeping."

He stared at Abu. "My charioteers are asleep?"

"Some sleeping potion, lord. In beer, we think."

It was one of the few times in his life that he bellowed. The household burst into action at the sound. Meren strode around his office, unable to keep still in his fury. The captain of charioteers rushed in, wiping the crumbs of his evening meal from his mouth.

Meren barked out orders for a search, directed the physician to attend the drugged men, and generally made sure his men would never take beer from a suspected murderer again. When he was finished, everyone but Abu retreated, thankful that they still possessed their skins and their heads.

"Abu, set a watch on the river in the direction of the artisans' village."

"But lord, surely even Imsety wouldn't be foolish enough to sail by night. The sandbars, the hippos—"

"A while ago I was sure my charioteers wouldn't allow themselves to be put to sleep by a possible murderer."

"Aye, lord."

"If they've gone to the village and they find Kysen—"

Meren lapsed into silence. He wrapped a hand around the back of his ebony chair and squeezed until it ap-

peared as if the bones of his knuckles would push
through the skin of his hand.

"If they find Kysen—"

15

The only confessions Kysen forced out of Thesh that afternoon were hundreds of minor transgressions involving tomb paintings, coffins, and statues for unreported customers. To his surprise, once Thesh admitted one sin, he burst forth with the others as a breached dike leaked water. Unfortunately, the scribe seemed to consider the wrath of the vizier a greater threat than Kysen had anticipated. When he threatened to reveal the villagers' dealings if Thesh didn't confess to the murder, the poor scribe burst into tears but remained stubbornly silent, and Kysen withdrew the threat before Thesh fainted.

So now here he was, back at his perch on the roof of Thesh's house, sitting up all night hugging his newfound views on the villagers in hopes of spying some illicit activity. He still suspected Thesh—and would until he proved who'd done the murder—but his view of the situation had changed after he'd overheard that conversation with Useramun.

Laying his head on the wall top, he closed his eyes for a moment. He'd been watching since the village had quieted for the night. No one stirred, and he was weary of looking at blank walls and listening to the screeches of the village cats. He heard a creak and lifted his head. Below, someone left the shelter of a doorway and glided around a house, Useramun's house, to the side stairs. That walk, that rolling glide. It was the painter.

Useramun crept upstairs to the roof and walked to the back of the house, which rested against the village wall. Kysen strained to see what the man was doing, but moonlight only aided his vision so far. Then he saw movement.

Useramun vanished over the wall. Kysen burst into quiet flight. In moments he was on Useramun's roof, creeping toward the wall. He reached it, cautiously peered over, and found a ladder. Beyond the foot of the ladder Useramun stumbled in the darkness after a distantly retreating light—a torch. Kysen waited for a count of twenty, then scrambled down the ladder after the painter.

Keeping the painter in sight and yet following at enough distance not to be heard when he stumbled over rocks proved difficult and painful. He heard Useramun grunt as he stepped on a jagged stone. Dropping behind a boulder, Kysen waited for his quarry to adjust his sandal. Then he crept after him once more. The torch climbed the hills that surrounded the village and descended again, following the northern path to the nobles' cemetery.

Kysen hated every step. Spirits roamed the western desert at night. Everyone knew that. So Useramun must have a powerful reason to venture forth, as did whoever he was following. Kysen's foot slipped on the loose rock at the base of a cliff. Pebbles clattered, but Useramun didn't turn. Kysen waited anyway, and as he waited a breeze whipped around the cliff, moaning and whining.

The sound filled the void of night and made Kysen shudder. Angry souls roamed the deserts—starving fiends, ancestors of those whose families had ceased to provide sustenance for them in the afterlife. Kysen gripped the dagger at his belt, knowing that it would do him no good should a spirit attack.

Best keep his mind on his quest. Useramun had rounded the base of a hill. Kysen staggered after him. As he skirted the slope, he expected to see the vague outline of the painter's kilt, but didn't. Cursing, he sped along a strip of flat land that turned into a track. It climbed another hill. Near the summit, Kysen dropped on his belly and crawled so that he could look over the side without revealing himself. No Useramun. Over the next hill he spied the bobbing torchlight, headed for a small cliff.

Useramun must still be following it. Kysen hurried down the hill after the light. On the floor of the valley he began to encounter rubble cast into hillocks and mounds. They were at the edge of the ruins of a temple from centuries ago in the time of the Pharaoh Sesostris. He walked more quickly now, for he couldn't see the light in the next valley, or Useramun. He walked past a broken limestone block, then slowed and turned back, drawing his dagger.

Resting against the base of the block was something white. Kysen sheathed his dagger and dropped to his knees beside Useramun. The painter lay still, his head lolling to the side, his legs splayed. Kysen could see something dark and wet on his head. He sniffed the coppery bitter smell of blood and leaned close. There was a gash in the back of the painter's head. Nearby lay a rock spattered with more blood.

Cursing, Kysen shifted the painter's body until it was supine, then bent over it to feel for the beat of life at his neck. Useramun groaned and opened his eyes. His arms came up, and he thrashed wildly at Kysen, who raised his own arm in defense.

"Damn you, be still."

"Seth?"

"Can you walk?"

"Don't know. They thought I was dead."

Kysen rose and dragged the painter upright. Useramun protested with a whimper, but remained standing.

"You listen to me," Kysen said as he steadied the
painter. "Find a place to hide. I'm going on, but I'll be
back to help you."

"You know? Be careful. They're not far ahead, at
Hormin's tomb."

"Gods, you're a fool to come after them alone."

"And you?"

"Shut your mouth and hide, painter."

Useramun's teeth flashed in the moonlight. He grimaced as he started toward a V-shaped indentation in
the hillside caused by an ancient flood, but swayed and
would have fallen if Kysen hadn't caught him. Kysen
thrust his shoulder under the painter's arm and walked
him toward the shelter. Useramun clung to him, and
Kysen swore again.

"If you weren't bleeding all over me, I'd think you'd
done this just to get me to touch you."

Useramun laughed and then gasped. Kysen lowered
him to the ground so that he nestled in the arms of the
V. Tearing the painter's kilt, he pressed the scrap of
linen to the wound.

"Hold that and stay still."

He left Useramun cradling his head and pleading not
to be left behind. He risked running to make up time,
but needn't have worried. The torch was still in sight. It
had nearly reached the small cliff, and had stopped by
the time Kysen slipped behind a fallen boulder a few
yards away from the sheer face of limestone.

A tomb entrance had been cut into the cliff, a rectangular opening roughly knocked out and ready to be smoothed by stoneworkers. The torch had been stuffed into a pile of rubble near the entrance, and beside it, her shift rippling in the desert wind, stood Beltis. As he watched, the concubine bent and picked up a sack at her feet before entering the tomb shaft. Vague light flickered from the entrance, indicating that lamps had been lit inside.

Priding himself on his insight, Kysen slithered out from behind his rock and over to the entrance. Rough steps had been hacked into the side of the cliff. He slipped inside. Putting his back to a wall, he edged down a few steps, then stopped as he heard Beltis.

"It was madness to light our way with that torch."

A man answered her in a slightly hysterical voice distorted by the echo off the tomb walls.

"I tell you I'm not chancing an encounter with demons," the man said. "Not again. Not after what I've done. I've suffered enough."

The voices retreated, still squabbling. Kysen eased down the stairs, past a supply of torches left by the tomb's excavators, until they graded into a steeply sloping downward walk. He stopped in a shadow when the shaft widened into an antechamber, a rectangular room that connected with the burial chamber through a recently cut entrance. Debris from the cut still lay in hastily made piles on either side of the opening.

From the burial chamber he could hear scraping and chipping noises, as if someone were hard at work excavating in the next room. When the noises started, Beltis and her ally had stopped arguing. Silence fell, and Kysen strained to hear anything at all. To his surprise, the light inside the burial chamber dimmed. He waited, but heard nothing further.

He was about to investigate when more scraping noises echoed in the chamber and the light there brightened again. Next he heard a clatter and more scrapes, this time coming toward him. He bolted for the ramp, scrambled up the stairs and into the open. Racing for his boulder, he dropped behind it and peeped over the top in time to see Beltis pop out of the tomb entrance, dragging her sack as if she'd stuffed it with rocks.

Behind her came a man, his arms laden with several boxes stacked on top of each other so that his face was hidden. He set them down in the pool of light cast by the torch, but he was too tall, and the light didn't reach his shoulders and head. Kysen cursed silently at the man for not offering him a clear view. He returned his gaze to the boxes and caught a glimpse of alabaster, sheet gold, and ebony. No Egyptian could mistake the sight.

The man picked up the boxes again while Beltis went ahead, grasping the torch, and dragged her sack. Again the man stayed just outside the pool of light. They set off down the trail by which they'd arrived, heading in the direction of the village.

Kysen watched them leave. Burdened as they were, he could catch up with them. He had to examine Hormin's tomb. There shouldn't have been anything in it to be removed. A dead man's possessions weren't placed in his eternal house until the day his body was brought for burial. He returned to the entrance and again lit one of the torches Beltis had stuck in a basin of sand. Whipping back down the shaft, he entered the burial chamber.

Undecorated, the chamber would soon hold the dead man's mummiform coffin. What caught Kysen's attention was the rectangular sarcophagus into which the coffin would be placed. Normally a scribe might expect to afford a wooden sarcophagus. Hormin had one of red granite—carved on all sides with images of the gods and inscribed with sacred texts.

Taking a moment to light three lamps, Kysen examined the sarcophagus. He ran his hand over the cool, polished surface of the granite. His fingers dipped into the grooves of the outline of a figure of a god. Shifting the lid would take the strength of at least four men. His hand skimmed over the rounded top of the lid as he walked around the container. He wondered if the objects Beltis and her companion had taken from the chamber had come from the sarcophagus. As he walked, his sandal slipped on the dusty floor. He tottered and glanced down to find he'd stepped in white grit at the base of the wall behind the sarcophagus.

Chunks and flakes of plaster lay scattered at the base of a hole in the wall. He'd found what he was looking for. He remembered that Hormin had decided to enlarge his tomb many days ago, only to abruptly change his mind again. Now he knew why; the hole, wide enough to admit a kneeling man, had been knocked into what should have been virgin rock. Instead, it cut into a cavity.

Kysen grasped one of the lamps, knelt before the hole, and eased it inside. The light touched metal and blazed. Kysen winced, squinted, and gasped. He breathed in a whiff of old air, dust, and the faint smell of wood and resin. He backed up, sat on his heels, and stared.

"Osiris protect me."

He shivered, licked his lips, and gathered his courage. Bending to prop himself on all fours, he stuck his head into the hole again and held the lamp out in front of his body. Gold shone back at him—a wall of gold. No, it was the side of a tall, gilded shrine of archaic design, one used to house coffins of royalty.

Kysen swallowed and leaned out. The hole had pierced the wall of an old tomb. The floor of the chamber lay several feet below, and Kysen levered himself inside to stand in front of the shrine. Around the chamber lay stacks of boxes that would contain food and clothing. He spotted a disassembled chariot. A bed stood nearby, its lion's-head finials grimacing at him. He saw stacks of weapons—spears, lances, bows, arrows. A man's tomb. He returned his gaze to the shrine.

The seal on the shrine had been broken and its doors stood ajar. Holding the lamp high, Kysen approached them. Within lay a sarcophagus of wood covered entirely in engraved sheet gold. Twisted and broken debris lay around its base. Its lid lay askew, exposing a nested set of coffins with the lids removed.

Kysen hovered in the threshold of the shrine and looked over the edge of the sarcophagus. He sucked in his breath as his gaze fastened on torn garlands, a blackened shroud. Beneath the torn shroud he glimpsed, inside the innermost of three coffins, an arm. A bandaged arm, torn from its crossed position over the breast, coated in solidified unguent.

His breathing had grown shallow and rapid, and as his glance flicked to the end of the arm, he backed up, for the hand had been partially torn from the wrist. He knew why. In a burial so rich, the most portable and valuable objects lay on the body itself—rings, bracelets, necklaces, amulets. Kysen shook his head, his stomach roiling at the sight of the desecrated body.

As he retreated in horror from the shrine, he felt a rush of air at his back. He turned, but not in time. Pain burst in his skull. For a moment he felt suspended in chaos. He dropped to his knees, fighting to remain conscious. His last sight was of the gold sarcophagus as he fell at its base.

Meren stood over the cowering figures on the floor of his office.

"May the gods curse your names," he said. "How far did you think to get in a skiff?"

He listened to Selket babble for a moment, then signaled to Abu to fetch a whip. Meren's patience had run out, and Imsety had yet to speak except to plead for mercy. Abu returned with a chariot whip and handed it to Meren.

Letting the lash uncurl to the floor, Meren gave it a preliminary flick. The leather snaked out, almost touching Selket. The air cracked.

Selket shrieked. "No!" She turned on her son. "This is your fault. If you hadn't been caught with that necklace—"

"But Djaper said the necklace was the answer to everything," Imsety whined.

Meren went still and snapped, "Why?"

Imsety ducked his head, stared at the ground, and said, "I don't know, lord. Because of its value? Please, I beg of you, believe me."

"Those were his very words? He said that the necklace was the answer?"

Imsety nodded and moaned.

"Be quiet."

Meren strode to his worktable, where he'd laid out the obsidian knife, the amulet, the empty *qeres* unguent jar, and the necklace.

He glanced up at his prisoners, who were still whimpering. "Take them to a cell."

Abu left with Imsety and Selket. Meren picked up the necklace and let the rows of beads trail from his fingers.

Red jasper, gold, lapis lazuli—a rich prize. Now that he'd found Imsety and his mother, he could take the time to have a royal jeweler examine it. The rows of beads alternated in bands of red, gold, and blue to form a collar that would fasten in the back. From the missing end pieces would hang a counterweight to balance the necklace and hold it in place.

Djaper had valued this necklace for more than the wealth it represented. He'd told Imsety it was the answer. The answer. Yet Beltis claimed that the necklace was hers.

Of course, the woman had lied about not awakening when Hormin had left her. Imsety had babbled about seeing her take leave of her master that night. No doubt Beltis also knew where Hormin was going the night he died. And she'd fled to the village of the tomb makers. Both she and Hormin had been at the village the day of his death. They'd visited his tomb.

Meren dropped into his chair, holding the necklace. His gaze traveled from it to the unguent jar. *Qeres*, the rare salve so valuable that only king and queen now possessed it. Once *qeres* had been the prized unguent of princes and nobles. A luxury coveted by lost generations.

His fist wrapped around the necklace and squeezed. Lost generations. Long ago, *qeres* would have been used during a prince's life—and taken with him to his eternal house for his pleasure in the next. And the amulet. Nebi had said that this amulet was made to be placed on a body, a wealthy body, in a tomb. This heart amulet belonged in a tomb; no doubt there was much *qeres* in old tombs.

Something was pinching his hand. Meren looked down to find himself strangling the broad collar, with its bands of color stiffened with spacer beads. Djaper had told Imsety that the necklace had been damaged and needed repair—its finials were missing—but the pinlike bars of gold at the unfinished ends bore no scratches, as one would expect if its falcon-head or lotus finials had once been attached. The surface of the pins was smooth, untouched, as if it had been intended to remain so.

Something niggled at him. Some recent memory. When he'd been with Nebi, the amulet maker had been certain that the *ib* had been intended for a body. He'd known by the way it was finished. The necklace, too, was finished peculiarly. It wasn't really broken. Perhaps it had never possessed end pieces or a counterpoise. If so, then it couldn't have been worn. Neither could the heart amulet—unless both the necklace and the amulet had been intended for someone who didn't need the completed jewelry.

The only person who doesn't need complete jewelry is a dead one—a jeweler makes incomplete pieces only when they are intended for the tomb.

Meren rose from his chair with the necklace dangling from his fingers. He stared vacantly at the obsidian embalming knife. And what of the place where Hormin had been killed? Was it not in the place of the dead? Tomb robbery. What better place to plot tomb robbery with one's fellow thieves than in the embalming sheds at night? And if Beltis knew of the looting, and if Beltis was in the tomb-makers' village, she either killed Hormin or knew who did.

Dropping the necklace on his worktable, Meren deliberately made himself go slowly. Hormin hadn't been taking bribes to gather his wealth, or hoarding the revenue from his farm. He'd been robbing tombs. Sacrilege. Perhaps the greatest of all crimes—desecration of the dead. One who committed such a transgression risked the curses of the gods and vengeance from the grave. But greed conquered most fears, in Meren's experience.

The risk, however, was so great that only rich tombs were worth it. Therefore the stakes were high, and the danger greater. The cemeteries were guarded day and night and robbery attempts rare, or so everyone thought. Yet Hormin had found a way to rob a tomb, most likely while at the tomb-makers' village. And it had gotten him killed.

It was time to go to the tomb-makers' village. The sun would rise in an hour or two; only then would it be safe to cross the river. Meren gripped the edge of the worktable and closed his eyes. Kysen slept in a village that contained a murderer, most likely more than one murderer.

It had been his own idea to send him there. Now he regretted his decision. The tomb robbers had killed three men already; he was certain they wouldn't stop at a fourth.

16

He descended upon the tomb-makers' village like a lion upon a herd of oryx. Storming down the path into the valley, his charioteers banged on the gates with their spears while he cursed the delay caused by the necessity of traveling by foot through the hills and cliffs. Someone opened the gates, and his charioteers thrust them back. Meren charged through them and stalked up to a man standing at the front of a crowd of villagers, who had dropped to their knees upon seeing his bronze and gold armor and weapons.

"I am the Eyes of Pharaoh. Where is my servant?"

The man bowed to him. "I know not, lord."

"Find him at once."

A search of the entire village failed to produce Kysen. Furious, Meren rounded on the man to whom he'd first spoken.

"Who else is missing? Quickly, fool."

"Th-the woman Beltis, a painter called Useramun, the sons of the coffin maker Pawero, the draftsman Woser. Others are in the Great Place for their shift."

Meren gripped the hilt of his dagger and spoke through his teeth. "Damn you, where have these people gone?"

"I know not, lord. Your servant retired as we all did. I thought he was asleep until you came."

"Who are you?"

"Thesh, lord, scribe of the village."

Abu emerged from a crowd of villagers pushing a man in front of him. This man supported another, who stumbled and whined as he walked.

"Ramose and Hesire, sons of Pawero, lord. I've questioned them and others. None of them knows where your servant is."

Meren's hand worked open and closed over his dagger hilt. He thought furiously. All of the missing villagers had had dealings with Hormin in making his tomb. The tomb. Tomb robbing. Apprehension turned to dread. His heart pounded against his ribs as he realized what must have happened. Kysen had found the murderer—or the murderer had found him.

"Thesh," he barked. "You will show me the way to Hormin's tomb at once."

They sped over the hills and across valleys of shale and limestone like shadows of wind-driven clouds. Each second, each moment when Thesh hesitated to take his bearings, stretched his control near to breaking. They raced down yet another hill into a valley sheltering the ruins of a temple.

Something moved behind a broken column, and Abu shouted. Drawing his sword, he thrust his body between Meren and the column as charioteers rushed past them. Charioteers pounced on a man leaning on the column and dragged him from behind it. Half-conscious, he slumped between two guards.

"Useramun?" Thesh stepped forward and shook the man's shoulder. "He's been hurt, lord."

As Thesh spoke, the painter slumped forward. The guards lowered him to the ground. Swearing, Meren directed them to take the painter back to the village. Without further delay he raced after Thesh, who clambered up another hill, only to drop to his knees at its summit. Meren joined him.

The scribe pointed. Dawn approached; with the sky lightening, he could make out a small cliff into which had been cut the entrance to a tomb. It appeared deserted.

Every moment he delayed risked Kysen's life, yet he couldn't rush down there with his men and warn his quarry. He would go himself. But what if no one was there? Shoving aside his fear, Meren signaled to Abu that he and the others should wait. He could see that Abu thought he should allow one of his men to explore, but he couldn't sit on this hill while his son was in danger.

Quietly, taking care not to dislodge rocks and pebbles, he worked down the hill and sped to the base of the cliff. Rushing the last few steps, he flattened himself against the side of the entrance. Torchlight flickered, and Meren said a prayer of thanks to the gods.

Drawing his dagger, he slithered inside. At the base of a set of stairs that led to a ramp, he paused, listening. Solid rock blocked off sounds from the outside, and he could hear nothing from the burial chambers below. A sputtering torch turned the limestone walls gold and the ceiling black. He put his foot on the ramp, and heard a woman shout.

"I told you to kill him, you fool!"

Then she screamed. Meren launched himself down the ramp. Running hard, he careened into an antechamber. The woman Beltis hurled herself out of the coffin chamber at the same time, and they crashed into each other. Meren grabbed her and hurled her aside as he heard a distant commotion.

He rushed into the coffin chamber. Nothing. He stood in front of a red granite sarcophagus, confused and desperate. As he looked wildly around the chamber, he heard the sounds of a fight again and then silence. Rounding the sarcophagus, he found a hole. He knelt and peered inside at rich destruction. A golden shrine lay before him, along with burial furniture, a chariot, wine jars, scattered jewelry, broken spears, and baskets.

To the left of the shrine was a gilded couch, which was occupied. Kysen! Kysen lay as if he'd fallen on the couch, his hands bound before him and his head bleeding from a wound at the back.

Wary, Meren waited, hardly daring to breathe, as he searched the lamplit chamber. He heard someone moving behind the shrine. Meren silently dropped down into the chamber and hugged the wall of the shrine. Edging toward the corner, he looked around it just as a man walked from behind it toward Kysen carrying an alabaster wine jar. His shoulder and arm muscles rippled as he raised the vessel above his head and aimed for Kysen.

Meren moved out from the shrine and cocked his dagger arm back, but the man turned suddenly and heaved the jar at him. Meren caught a brief glimpse of his face before the jar hit him. Woser! The vessel hit Meren's arms as he threw them up to protect his face. The blow sent Meren staggering backward, stunned, to land on the floor by the shrine.

He sat up and shook his head. Across the room, the draftsman sprang at Kysen, who dodged aside and tripped the man. Falling, Woser lashed out and gripped Kysen's ankle as he tried to flee. Kysen fell, but rolled and kicked Woser in the stomach. The draftsman grunted, curling in on himself for a moment, while Kysen turned and crawled toward Meren.

Meren had managed to grip one of the doors of the shrine to lever himself upright. As he did so, Woser pounced on Kysen. Meren watched his son fall halfway between the couch and the shrine.

Woser wrapped his arms around Kysen, and they rolled across the floor over fragments of broken jars and furniture. Meren took a step toward them and staggered against the shrine again, dizzy. When he regained his balance, he saw Woser straddling his son.

The draftsman had the end of a broken spear in his hands. Kysen gripped Woser's wrists in both hands and was holding off a death blow with fading strength. Wiping the blood from his eyes, Meren spied his dagger lying on the threshold of the shrine.

He dove for it, stood, and hurled it at Woser. There was a loud thud as the point embedded itself in Woser's bare back. The draftsman jerked, then froze; the spear in his hands quivered. Then Kysen shoved hard, and he toppled sideways. Meren stumbled over to Kysen, who lay on his back half-pinned by Woser's body. Shoving the dead man aside, Meren lifted Kysen into his arms.

"You're all right?" Meren asked.

Kysen's voice was weak. "He was going to shut me up in here."

Behind them Abu dropped from the hole into the burial chamber and rushed to them. Kneeling, he peered from Meren to Kysen.

"No lectures," Meren said. "I shouldn't have come without you."

"Aye, lord. We have the woman."

"Then help us out of here, man. I've had enough of— damn."

Kysen slumped in his arms. Meren laid him on the floor, and Abu probed the wound at the back of his head.

"He's weak from loss of blood, lord, but he will recover. You know how head wounds bleed."

"If he dies, I'll flay that woman alive, with a flint knife."

"Yes, lord, but he's not going to die."

"Good, because I've already killed this night, and I've no stomach for more."

Refusing to leave Kysen in the care of Thesh and his wife, Meren sailed downriver with him to the royal precincts. From the dock he summoned a litter, and soon he had deposited his son in bed, Beltis in a cell, and himself in his own chamber. He left orders for Hormin's wife and son to be held until he could assure himself that they, too, hadn't been involved in the looting of the rich tomb.

Having left men to guard it, he could afford a few hours' sleep after receiving assurance from his physician that Kysen's wound wasn't serious. Like the dregs of old beer, echoes of fear for Kysen disturbed his sleep. He awoke bleary-eyed and apprehensive. Only a visit to his sleeping son's room dispelled his anxiety.

His first act was to dispatch runners to the palace and the Place of Anubis announcing the capture and death of the murderer of Hormin, for he had no doubt that Woser had been the killer. A full explanation would have to be extracted from Beltis, however. He didn't look forward to the ordeal. Talking to Beltis left him feeling soiled.

It was also urgent that he find out whether, by some curious happenstance, Hormin and the others had been involved with the queen's treason. The possibility was remote, but real. As he dined on shat cakes and roast duck followed by figs and grapes, he was preparing to send for Beltis when Kysen walked in, carefully, trailed by Remi's nurse, Mutemwia. She waved an ostrich-feather fan at Kysen and shook a sistrum.

"Out, out, demons of the dead."

Kysen winced as the little cymbals mounted on the sistrum chimed. He cast a glance of appeal at Meren, who clapped his hands for silence. Mutemwia subsided, but muttered charms under her breath.

"I'm sure Kysen values your concern and care for him, Mut, but you're hurting his head."

"Better a sore head than one possessed by a dead spirit."

"Mut, you may conduct your spells and charms in Kysen's bedchamber, but not in his face."

Mut bowed. "As you wish, lord."

After she left, Meren dragged his ebony chair to rest before the worktable, found a cushion for it, and pointed. Kysen sat, grimacing as he lowered his body. Meren leaned on the worktable and surveyed his son. Kysen was pale, and his eyes had violet smudges beneath them, but he appeared strong.

"How are you?" Meren asked.

"A thousand fiends of the underworld are dancing on drums in my head."

"You are supposed to be in bed."

"I know you must have the truth from Beltis, and I know part of it, perhaps enough to shake her."

"Don't you think all these hours spent alone in a cell will have intimidated her?"

"In truth, Father, I suspect she's used the time to think up lies to save herself. But I may be able to rout her."

"Very well." Meren sent for Beltis and returned to Kysen. "I'm doing this because you won't rest easily until we have the whole truth, and because I must know for certain that this *qeres* unguent came from that tomb and isn't a royal or sacred supply." He quickly told Kysen about the queen's treason and the unguent.

As he finished, Abu entered and stepped aside to al-

low the concubine Beltis to come in. A guard behind
the woman shoved her into the room and shut the door
while Abu took up a scribe's kit from a shelf and squat-
ted on the floor so that his kilt stretched tightly across
his lap. Placing a piece of papyrus on this surface, he
inked his reed pen and waited.

Beltis hadn't noticed Abu. She was glancing from
Meren to his son and back again, her lower lip caught
between her teeth. Meren let the silence stretch out.
This woman had almost killed Kysen, and he was having a difficult time restraining the desire to strangle her
and cast her into the desert for the vultures and hyenas
to devour her flesh.

He noted with satisfaction that her upper lip was
sweaty. She toyed with a bracelet at her wrist with
quick, jerky movements. At last she burst out in speech.

"Woser forced me to come with him!"

Meren only lifted one brow and continued to stare at
her.

"He planned it all," she rushed on, "days ago, he
planned it all. Hormin wanted another room in his
house of eternity, and when the laborer began cutting
the back wall to test the strength of the rock, he
knocked through the side of another tomb. But I knew
nothing of this until Hormin told me, the day before he
died."

Kysen glanced at Meren. "That, at least, is probably
true."

Meren tapped his fingers on the worktable, ignored
Beltis, and mused, "I seem to remember that a laborer
fell to his death in the Great Place recently."

Beltis skewed her gaze away from him, but he
waited.

After another few moments, Beltis's endurance broke
again. "Hormin told me he made Woser kill him. He

didn't trust the laborer, and anyway he didn't want to—"

"Share?" Kysen asked.

"Yes." Beltis cast a sideways glance through eyes that had almost closed. "But I knew how great a sin he'd committed. I knew it was wrong, and all along I urged my master to relent and seal the old tomb. But he wouldn't listen to me. I prayed day and night to the gods, but he wouldn't listen. Woser was to take jewels and other valuable things from the tomb and bring them to Hormin at the Place of Anubis."

"He went, but never came back with the jewels," Kysen said. "You must have been furious to find him dead and the riches gone."

"But I didn't kill him," Beltis said, her face lighting up with triumph. "You know who did. I'm innocent."

Meren laughed and shoved himself away from the worktable. He walked around Beltis, inspecting her dirty shift and dusty hair. She pursed her lips. He knew she wanted to spit at him and dared not.

"Innocent of Hormin's death, perhaps."

"I don't understand," she said.

"I see you've forgotten that Bakwerner and Djaper are also dead."

"Also killed by Woser in his mad efforts to conceal his guilt," Beltis said smoothly.

Meren glanced at Kysen, who leaned back in his chair and smiled at Beltis. The woman stirred uneasily at this sign of contentment.

"Father, do you know how active our Beltis has been at the village?"

"No," Meren said. "Do tell me."

"Our Beltis is a locust. She hops from man to man. And she wanted me to see her do it. She flaunted her relations with Useramun the painter and with Thesh and Woser. And then she came to me."

Meren lowered his lashes so that he didn't reveal his anger to the concubine. The thought of that woman interfering with Kysen fed his wrath and disgust with her.

"Possibly," Kysen went on, "possibly she thought I would wilt like a plucked lotus once she'd bedded me. A stupid presumption, but then her experience is limited."

"It is not!"

"For after she'd gone and I overheard Useramun and Thesh, I began to think about all of us—all of us favored by the concubine." Kysen listed the names on his fingers. "Hormin she used for what he could provide. But the others, Useramun and Thesh, they are men of appeal, each in his own way. When she went to the tomb-makers' village, she could enjoy herself with men of much greater beauty than her master. Even I am more pleasing than Hormin."

Beltis gave them a complacent smile, which vanished at Kysen's next words.

"But not Woser."

Meren laughed as he perceived Kysen's reasoning. "Not Woser indeed. Skinny, beak-nosed, lacking in wealth."

"Yes," Kysen said. "If you were to stand us in a line, we who have been favored, Woser alone does not belong. I knew Beltis tolerated Hormin because of his possessions rather than his appearance. She favored Useramun and Thesh for their beauty, for they offered her no wealth. Woser certainly wasn't going to change his looks." Here Kysen paused to watch Beltis wipe perspiration from her chin. "But perhaps he offered something else."

"Your head is broken," Beltis said with a sniff. "These are fancies of sickness."

"After I realized how solicitous you'd been to a man you ordinarily wouldn't allow near your rubbish heap, I decided to watch you more closely. But you slipped out of the village last night without me seeing you. Perhaps with the aid of a ladder as did Useramun. But I did see the painter, who suspected you of killing Hormin. He followed you. I followed him."

"I told you," Beltis said, her voice rising. "He forced me to come with him."

"You forget," Kysen said. "I saw you, and more importantly, I heard you. You were the one giving the orders. Looting that tomb was your idea. And in any case, I'm sure he told you about the tomb when he gave you the broad collar."

Beltis shook her head. Kysen stood up and faced her.

"Hormin had promised you more riches, and you weren't going to let a small detail like his death separate you from them. Woser feared demons more than scorpions or the plague. But you didn't, and you browbeat him and cajoled him and threatened him until he consented to help you steal from that tomb."

"I didn't."

Meren joined Kysen in standing over Beltis.

"Odd," he said. "Kysen, didn't you tell me that Woser said as much while he was in the tomb with you?"

Kysen nodded, then winced as the movement pained him.

Meren folded his arms over his chest and mused. "Didn't you tell me that she threatened to reveal that Woser killed Hormin?"

"Yes, Father."

"Which made Woser feel most ill-used, considering that he hadn't meant to kill Hormin in the first place."

"Lies!"

Kysen sneered at the woman. "Woser was too frightened to lie. Every moment in that tomb was agony to a man as terrified of spirits and demons as Woser."

Meren began to stalk Beltis, sensing her fear and slipping control. She backed away from him, protesting her innocence.

"Woser was puke-scared. So puke-scared that he couldn't leave his bed the last few days—especially after his fight with Hormin at the Place of Anubis. Which means he couldn't have gone to Hormin's house and killed Bakwerner or Djaper. He didn't even know that those two were a threat. That leaves you, Beltis. You knew Bakwerner made a scene and said that he knew things. He wasn't speaking of the old tomb, but you panicked and killed him in case he'd discovered something."

Beltis backpedaled as Meren came at her, shaking her head.

"Woser was sick," Meren said as he moved toward the concubine. "He didn't know that Djaper had discerned the significance of that broad collar. Djaper found out, didn't he? Clever, clever Djaper reasoned it out. He knew the collar was made incomplete on purpose for inclusion in a burial."

Beltis backed into a shelf on the wall and edged away from Meren.

"He wanted a share, didn't he?" Meren asked. "He told you he knew about the necklace, and that he wanted a share. Did he want too much? Or couldn't you stomach sharing at all once you realized Hormin was gone?"

Meren said this last as he backed Beltis into a corner.

She yelped. "No!"

Kysen sighed and carefully reseated himself in Meren's chair. "I grow weary and bored, Father. Let us stick hot brands on her face until she bleats out the truth."

Both he and Meren covered their ears at the shriek that issued from Beltis's red lips. In a heart's beat Abu was recording the true tale of the death of Hormin the scribe.

$\triangledown$

17

That evening Meren left the barracks where Beltis was imprisoned, weary and yet relieved. He had most of the truth now, and the woman had confirmed his suspicion that neither she nor any of the others were in the service of the queen. He went to Kysen's room, where he found his son saying good-night to Remi.

Kysen lay on his bed, to which he'd been sent once Beltis had broken, with Remi sitting beside him. The child made roaring noises as he marched a wooden hippopotamus up Kysen's stomach and pulled the string that moved the creature's mouth open and closed. Meren saw Kysen wince as Remi shrieked, and scooped the child up in his arms along with the toy.

"Time for bed."

"Aaaaarrrrrrgh."

Remi poked Meren's nose with the hippo. Mutemwia appeared with a tray of wine and bread, set it down, and took Remi.

"Bid your father and the lord good-night," she said to Remi.

The child jumped from Mutemwia's arms, wobbled, then executed a precarious bow.

"Peaceful sleep to you."

Meren tried not to smile as Kysen accepted this

courtly behavior with solemnity. He inclined his head at
the boy.

"A fine bow, Remi."

The boy grinned, then roared again and toddled out
of the room.

Meren dragged a stool to the bed and sat beside
Kysen. He poured wine for himself, but Kysen refused,
saying that the physician forbade him to drink anything
but water for two more days. His bed, like Meren's, sat
within a shelter made of a delicate gilt wood frame set
upon a dais. He lay back on the cushions and stared at
the filmy hangings that billowed out from the frame in
the evening breeze coming through the doors, which lay
open to the veranda and the garden beyond.

"Have you gotten the truth from her?" he asked
Meren.

"Most of it, I think."

"Then tell me, how did poor, terrified Woser ever
manage to kill Hormin?"

Meren sighed and sloshed his wine around in its
bronze goblet. "Only Woser and that laborer were in the
tomb when Hormin insisted upon testing the rock for
another chamber. When they broke into that tomb,
Woser wanted to seal it back up at once, but Hormin
persuaded him that they could use magic to protect
themselves while they looted it. They began on the
body, tearing away the amulets and spells that protected
the owner from harm."

"Woser lived in fear of spirits and demons," Kysen
said. "He seemed to think they reserved their most horrible punishments for him alone."

"Yes, and even though they tried to destroy the dead
man's ability to avenge himself, Woser remained terrified of his wrath. Hormin, with his usual lack of pity
and love of tormenting those weaker than himself,

taunted Woser with his fears. He would tease him that the dead prince was going to leave the tomb and come after Woser. Beltis heard him do this more than once the day he took her to see his tomb and his secret hoard."

Kysen rolled his eyes. "A stupid thing to do since he needed Woser to help him hide the valuables when they removed them. They were going to put them in Woser's family tomb, weren't they?"

Meren nodded as he tore a piece of bread from a loaf and bit into it. Swallowing, he continued. "The day he died, Hormin and Beltis fought as she said. He made the mistake of giving her that broad collar and thinking she'd be satisfied with it. But she wasn't, and they quarreled. As was her custom, she fled to the tomb-makers' village. When he came for her, she threatened to leave him. To keep her, he allowed her to see the old tomb and its treasure. She stayed, of course. But Woser was growing more and more terrified. So terrified that he became ill.

"Anyway, to keep Beltis satisfied, Hormin decided to give her a few more of the dead prince's baubles. Then he told Woser to meet him secretly that night at the Place of Anubis and bring the unguent, which Beltis had admired, and some gold rings that were on the prince's fingers."

"We found no gold rings at the Place of Anubis."

"Because Woser couldn't bring himself to touch the body again. Each time he went to the tomb, he suffered torments, fearing that the dead man would cast him into the underworld at any moment. He was certain that the Devourer would eat his soul. So he took only the unguent. Beltis got the truth from him when she returned to the village after Hormin's death. When Woser arrived at the embalming shed, Hormin was furious that he hadn't brought the rings. With his usual lack of judgment, he told Woser he was a coward and an ass."

"Hardly cause to stick a knife in a man."

"But Hormin went further," Meren said as he stared into his wine. "He knew that Woser feared the protective spells and curses on the dead prince's amulets and the coffin and the tomb walls."

Meren set down his goblet, pulled a folded piece of papyrus from his belt, and handed it to Kysen. "To protect himself and distract the wrath of the gods and the dead man, he left that in the coffin. It's a letter to the prince. In it he names Woser as its desecrator."

Kysen opened the letter and read. When he finished, he dropped it and whistled. "By all the gods, what an infernal bastard Hormin was."

"Aye. There's nothing more dangerous than a frightened and cornered animal. I don't understand why Hormin didn't realize what a risk he took. That night at the Place of Anubis, the fool told Woser about the letter—there in the place of the dead. Poor Woser went mad with fear and finally killed his tormentor."

Kysen shook his head in disbelief. "And all along, Beltis has been trying to preserve the secret of the prince's tomb. That's why she killed Bakwerner when he blundered into Hormin's house that day saying he knew things."

"She slipped out of the house while Bakwerner was fighting with the family and my men were distracted. She followed him to the office of records and tithes and killed him. Probably all Bakwerner really saw was the brothers watching Hormin depart for the Place of Anubis. His real aim must have been to get rid of the talented Djaper."

Kysen glanced at Meren's goblet. "And it would be

easy for her to poison Djaper's wine for the same reason, and then saunter over to the tomb-makers' village."

"Where she seduced Woser into returning to the prince's tomb," Meren said. "Do you know how she finally persuaded him? She promised him that they would burn the letter Hormin left and replace it with another blaming Hormin and calling down the wrath of the gods on the scribe's soul, which was already on its journey to the netherworld."

Kysen sank down in his pillows and groaned. "Fools. All of them, they were fools."

"I suppose they thought they could deceive the gods."

"Is that possible?" Kysen asked.

"I don't know, Ky, but I doubt it." Meren rose and glanced out at the garden. There was little time left before nightfall. "I must see the king this evening. He requested specifically to be informed about this murder. He's feeling trapped and restrained again. And there is this matter of the *qeres* unguent. He'll have to know about it, even if it proved a coincidence."

Meren paused, thinking. "Ky, there is evil news from the court concerning the queen. There is danger to the king. I can't explain it, but I've this foreboding, this vague fear that has no real foundation that I can perceive. Tomorrow we must speak of it."

Kysen nodded as he closed his eyes. "I thought you looked worried. I thank the gods I wasn't born royal."

"I do too." Meren smiled at his son. "Sleep well, Ky."

Hours later, Meren was admitted into the king's bedchamber through a concealed entrance guarded by tall Nubians. Tutankhamun was alone except for one body servant helping him undress, who lifted a heavy wig

from the king's head. Tutankhamun sighed and run
the curls that refused to be suppressed by weighty he.
dresses and crowns. Meren went to his knees before the
boy.

Tutankhamun frowned at him. "Where have you
been? I sent for you this afternoon."

"Thy majesty is right to chastise me, but I have been
pursuing thy enemies."

"Oh, leave off the ceremony. You're not hiding from
me behind it."

"Yes, majesty." Meren straightened and sat on his
heels. "I was pursuing the murderer of the Place of
Anubis."

Tutankhamun cast a gold belt at his servant and
whirled on Meren. "You caught him! Tell me everything."

While the king undressed, Meren told the story of
Hormin, Woser, and Beltis. When he finished, the king
sighed.

"I wish I could have been there for the fight."

"Gods preserve me from such an occurrence. Thy
majesty mustn't expose his sacred life for such petti-
ness."

"My majesty is sick of ambassadors and banquets
and especially of harems and wives."

The king vanished into his bathing chamber, and
Meren heard the sloshing of water. Meren glanced about
the room for the second time. He always inspected a
room as he entered it. One never knew what dangers lay
in even the most protected rooms in the kingdom.
Bright tiles shone at him from the walls, white and deep
Nile blue. Transparent hangings fluttered from the bed
canopy. He glimpsed a vigilant royal guard at each corner. They stood in the shadows, spears at the ready, pa-
tient, silent.

o few guards. The king must have dismissed the
ers. And only one servant. Was there greater safety
having many servants or one? Meren and the vizier
debated this point periodically. Outside, between the
white lengths of two columns, he could see a reflection
pool, and beside it a long black shadow reclining in the
silver light of the moon's rays. The king's leopard—Sa,
the guardian.

Meren shook his head. Why was he so on edge?
More so than usual after a fight or a resolved mystery.
The king emerged from the bathing chamber, a cloth
wrapped around his hips, his servants trailing him with
pots of oil and unguent. Without glancing at Meren or
the servant, Tutankhamun headed for the reflection
pool. He dropped onto an ebony and gold couch, sighing as he propped himself on the cushions. Meren
caught up with him and sank to the ground beside him.

"Now may we speak," the king said.

Meren glanced at the servant and recognized him. A
Libyan captive, he'd been taken in battle before reaching puberty. He was deaf. The vizier had trained him to
serve the king and given him the name Teti.

"I will go to the Controller of the Mysteries tomorrow and spin the tale of Hormin and his concubine,"
Meren said.

"Tomorrow I must fight with the High Priest of
Amun about taxes. He wants all of mine as well as his.
The old jackal."

Meren hesitated, then said, "You have spoken to the
queen?"

Tutankhamun turned on his back and stared up at the
leaves of a palm tree while his servant rubbed his legs
with oil.

"I did," he said. "She stared deep into my eyes. Not
once did she look away or flinch, and she denied every-

thing. Said it was a plot to keep us apart and preve
from living in harmony and producing child.
Ankhesenamun has always been an excellent liar."

Teti took one of the king's hands and began workin,
oil into the fingers and palm.

"You pretended to believe her?" Meren asked.

"Yes." Tutankhamun glanced at him and grinned.
"I've learned much since we began. Have I not?"

"Thy majesty possesses the cunning of the hyena and
the bravery of the lion."

"My majesty knows drivel when his ears are covered
with it."

Meren bowed from his sitting position. "Pardon,
sire."

"I pretended remorse at suspecting her of treason and
rewarded her with that palace. She was furious, but
couldn't show it, since I was rewarding her. She leaves
as soon as we can replace her servants."

"I suppose the messenger who was caught with the
letter to the Hittite king is dead."

"Killed trying to escape," the king said.

Meren listened to the king's tale of the capture of the
messenger on the northeastern border. Teti finished with
his oil and produced an obsidian jar. Removing its stop-
per, he inhaled the scent of the unguent. Meren turned
toward the young man as he scooted closer to the king
so that he could apply the salve to the king's hands and
neck. Teti held the jar in one hand, dipped a small ivory
spoon into the unguent, and reached out to the king.
Meren sniffed, and smelled myrrh and spice. Myrrh and
spice.

With a cry, Meren lurched forward and knocked
Teti's hands aside. The servant fell backward. The jar
flew from his hand, crashed on the tiles that bordered
the reflection pool, and splintered. Across the pool, Sa

:opard sprang to his feet and loped toward them.

king shot up from his couch as Meren threw him-

.f between Tutankhamun and Teti.

"Meren! Are you mad?"

Guards darted at them even as the king spoke. Meren shoved the king so that his body blocked Tutankhamun from the servant and pointed at Teti.

"Take him."

Sa joined them and snaked his body around the king's legs. Teti made gasping sounds as two men grabbed his arms and shoved him to his knees. He darted bewildered glances from his captors to Meren.

"You're scaring him," the king said as he peered at the young man from behind Meren.

"A moment, majesty."

Assured that the servant was under control, Meren went to the edge of the pool and retrieved a fragment of the obsidian jar. He picked up a fallen palm leaf, tore it, and placed the fragment on it so that his skin didn't come in contact with the unguent. Calling for a lamp, he took it from the guard and read the engraved inscription on the fragment. His lips folded together and he swore under his breath.

Returning to the king, he handed Tutankhamun the palm leaf and jar fragment. He held the lamp so that the king could examine the inscription.

The king read it and handed the leaf back to Meren. "I don't understand. The unguent is from the treasury of the god Amun."

"This is *qeres*, majesty."

"Isn't that the unguent—"

"The unguent coveted by the Great Royal Wife."

"Ankhesenamun," the king said.

They both looked at the silently weeping Teti.

Tutankhamun restrained Meren when he would approach the servant.

"Let me. He's frightened and doesn't understand."

Dismissing the guards, the king went to Teti, who fell to his knees and placed his cheek on the king's foot. The king knelt and raised his servant. While Meren watched, they conducted a silent conversation using hand signs. Tutankhamun gestured several times toward the unguent jar fragment.

When he finished, the king placed his hand on Teti's shoulder. The servant began to weep again, but kissed the hem of the king's kilt. Giving the young man several reassuring pats on the shoulder, he sent the servant away.

Tutankhamun rejoined Meren. "He knows little. It's as I thought. The chief bath attendant is responsible for making sure my supplies of salves and unguents are in place each day. The trays of jars were checked this morning and restocked from the palace storeroom. This jar appeared for the first time then."

Meren lowered his voice so that only the king could hear him. "Majesty, the queen requested *qeres* from the treasury not long ago. And there are no stores of it in the palace."

"I am to be astonished?"

"No, divine one. But we may thank the golden Horus for the queen's bad luck. If I hadn't been making inquiries about the unguent for this murder in the Place of Anubis, I would never have noticed that *qeres*."

"It's poisoned."

"Perhaps. I think so. There is a bitter smell to it that shouldn't be there."

The king's leopard yawned and strolled away. Tutankhamun lapsed into silence. He and Meren gazed at the pattern of moonbeams dancing over the surface of the water in the reflection pool.

"The queen again," Tutankhamun said in a whisper.

"Perhaps not."

"Not?"

Meren shrugged as he stood beside the king. "It came from the treasury of Amun."

"But to send poison in a container marked with the god's name, it is too absurd. The high priest would never make such a mistake."

"Unless he meant to," Meren said.

They both thought for a moment.

"We will examine the *qeres*, majesty. For poison."

"And then put it someplace secret."

"Yes, majesty."

"And then tell that old jackal that we have it."

"Thy majesty is wise."

"My majesty wants to live, Meren."

Meren turned to the king. "The Eyes of Pharaoh will do his best to see to it, majesty."

They both turned again to gaze out at the light-spattered water. Meren heaved a deep sigh and looked down at the scar on his wrist, his own personal legacy from a dead pharaoh. Keeping the king alive was a far more difficult and dangerous task than solving the murder in the Place of Anubis.